HULL LIBRARIES

Guns Across the
Rio Grande

When Captain Barnabas Quinnell, late of the defeated Confederate army, decides to smuggle rifles into Mexico, it seems like a simple, straightforward and profitable enterprise. He hasn't counted, though, on the Mexican officer who had been charged with putting an end to such gun-running. When Colonel Lopez and Captain Quinnell come face to face, only one of them will emerge alive from the bloody confrontation.

By the same author

Blood for Blood
Chisholm Trail Showdown

Guns Across the Rio Grande

Jack Tregarth

A Black Horse Western

ROBERT HALE

© Jack Tregarth 2016
First published in Great Britain 2016

ISBN 978-0-7198-2044-1

The Crowood Press
The Stable Block
Crowood Lane
Ramsbury
Marlborough
Wiltshire SN8 2HR

www.crowood.com

Robert Hale is an imprint
of The Crowood Press

Typeset by
Derek Doyle & Associates, Shaw Heath
Printed and bound in Great Britain by
CPI Group (UK) Ltd, Croydon, CR0 4YY

CHAPTER 1

'And they say that the Yankees will be here within a month. Is that true, Colonel?'

'The Americans? Coming here to Mexico City? Why, Princess, you are better informed than our military intelligence! No, President Johnson has better things to do than come here meddling in our poor country's affairs.'

The last waltz of the evening was drawing to a close and Colonel Lopez was sweeping Princess Marie de Polignac around the ballroom with great panache. They were speaking French, the accepted language of diplomacy and love, for which reason the colonel was exceedingly careful in what he said. The Emperor's ears were everywhere and the city was full of French officers who would be only too glad to denounce Lopez for being politically unreliable. He had many enemies in the capital: men who were jealous of his influence and power.

It was the summer of 1865. Everywhere one went in Mexico the talk was the same: would the

Americans invade again, as they had done less than twenty years earlier? When the French had installed their puppet Maximilian as Emperor of Mexico, barely eighteen months previously, the United States had still been at war with itself and in no fit state to object to a European monarch being foisted on a neighbouring country at gunpoint.

The War Between the States had now been over for four months though, and there were those in Washington who were looking south, wondering what might be done to topple the preposterous figure of the second Emperor of Mexico from his throne and to show Europe once for all that interference in the affairs of the North American continent would no longer be tolerated.

At about the same time as Colonel Lopez was flirting with a minor member of the Imperial House of France, indulging in verbal fencing that promised to end later that night in her boudoir, events were taking place some 700 miles to the north of Mexico City that would have a far greater impact on the colonel's future than the hour or two he would soon be spending in the bed of a beautiful woman.

The shabby and insignificant settlement of Pike's Landing lay on the south bank of the Pecos River. It was a debatable point whether the little hamlet was in the State of Texas or the New Mexico Territory. As a consequence of this uncertainty, neither Texas nor New Mexico showed any great enthusiasm for taking responsibility for Pike's Landing and enforcing the law there. This made the town a perfect haunt for all manner of men who preferred to conduct their activities away from the watchful eyes of sheriffs and marshals. It was accordingly the ideal location for the kind of dubious scheming that was taking place in Pike's Landing's only saloon on the evening of Saturday, 5 August 1865.

Captain Barnabas Quinnell, late of the Confederate Army, had come to the town with three of his men to meet a trooper of the US Cavalry who was minded to sell information about the planned dispositions of his unit – in return, of course, for a monetary reward. Ostensibly at least, the sticking point lay in what sum would satisfy the fellow.

Scripture tells us that Judas Iscariot was content to betray Christ for a mere thirty pieces of silver, but Trooper Thomas Jackson seemed to think that his own treachery was of considerably greater import than that of Judas; that it deserved a good deal more than the price paid for the life of Our Lord and saviour. In short, he was holding out for one hundred silver dollars. Quinnell gave the impression of a man not inclined to part with more than half that amount as he reasoned the case out to the cavalryman:

'We know those rifles are passing through some time soon. Tell you the truth, I'm not sure that we need give you a cent. The fifty dollars I'm offering – well, I'd call that downright handsome.'

Seeing any profit at all from his base actions beginning to slip away, Jackson became pugnacious.

'You and your boys don't want to get stingy, Captain. I know a thing or two. If nothin' else, it'd be well worth your while to stop up my mouth with some cash money, less'n I start thinking' 'bout telling some officer what I know.'

Nobody loves a traitor and Jackson was an especially unlovely example of the breed. Quinnell gazed long and hard at the mean-looking fellow for a space, until Trooper Jackson grew uncomfortable and averted his eyes.

'Fair's fair,' he said in a whining voice. 'I only want a good price for what I sell. Ain't nothin' wrong in that.'

Sweat glistened on the man's face as he recalled that he had come here, twenty miles from base and wearing civilian clothing, in order to strike this bargain. If Quinnell and his men wished, they could probably cut his throat after he left here and nobody would be any the wiser. Maybe he would do well to take what was offered. A hundred dollars would be no use to him if he were dead.

Some of what was going through Jackson's mind was plain to the man watching him. At last, when he was sure that the treacherous little skunk was thoroughly frightened, Quinnell spoke again.

'Very well, a hundred it shall be. But for that we require every last detail of the journey that those weapons will be making. And God help you if you play us false!'

Thomas Jackson felt relief washing through him like a healing draught. The tension eased away and he knew that he had won his gamble.

'The wagons will be heading north this coming Thursday,' he said. 'I don't call to mind the precise hour that they'll be leaving the base, most likely at about eight in the morning.'

'That's the spirit,' said Quinnell encouragingly. 'Will it just be rifles and ammunition? No Gatlings, I suppose?'

'No sir, just four hundred Henry repeaters, along with two thousand rounds of ammunition.'

'How many carts?'

'Just the one. The rifles and ammunition weigh a ton and a half.'

'What will the escort be?'

'Only a half-dozen men. The commandant's not looking for trouble. It's only twenty miles from the base to the arsenal at Las Cruces. They's treatin' it like a Sunday-school picnic.'

'There's nothing wrong with those rifles?'

'Not a bit of it. Just that with the war being over, they don't need 'em all down here any more. They're a-goin' to hand them over to the militia in Colorado.'

Barnabas Quinnell rubbed his jaw meditatively. Everything seemed almost too good to be true.

'And you're certain sure that they'll be taking the straight road, through the defile at San Angelo?' he queried.

'Sure,' said Jackson. 'It's the only way to Las Cruces, 'less'n you want to take the mule track through the hills.'

'Well, I reckon you've told us about all we need to know,' said Quinnell, smiling appreciatively, 'We are all obliged to you. I guess you'll be wanting your payment now, if I'm not mistook?'

'We settled on a hundred dollars, I think?'

'So we did, Mr Jackson, so we did. Come outside and I'll hand over the cash.'

Jackson looked uneasy at this suggestion, which provoked Captain Quinnell to mirth.

'You think I carry a heap of cash on my person every day?' he asked, laughing. . . . 'Not so. I've got your reward in the saddle-bag of my horse. Out in the barn, just across the way from here.'

He got to his feet and the three men sitting with him at the table did likewise. Thomas Jackson too stood up and followed the four others as they left the saloon.

It was pitch dark outside, Pike's Landing not having anything in the way of public lighting. Some illumination was to be had from the light spilling from windows, but it was not sufficient to make the streets of the little town easy to negotiate on moon-less nights such as this.

Quinnell took the trooper's arm in an amicable fashion, to guide him across to the barn. As they reached it one of the other men lit a storm lantern that was standing on the buckboard of a wagon. The feeble glow from this lamp barely touched the cav-ernous interior of the barn.

'Well, Mr Jackson,' said Quinnell, relinquishing the other man's arm and extending his hand, 'I suppose all that remains is to congratulate you on making a good deal for yourself.'

Instinctively the trooper took Quinnell's hand and shook it.

Then things moved exceedingly fast. Quinnell gripped the proffered hand very hard and also clamped his left hand around Jackson's wrist, holding him fast. As he did this another of his men grabbed the trooper's left arm and held it tightly.

'Hey, what's the idea?' Jackson said in a quavering voice. Then he realized precisely what the idea was. 'Listen,' he added, in a desperate attempt to talk his way out of the deadly trap into which he had fallen, 'I'll settle for the fifty dollars, if that's what this is about. Hell, just let me free and you can forget about paying me a cent!'

'No,' said Captain Quinnell gently and almost regretfully, 'it isn't the money. We couldn't let you go back to your base knowing what has been planned. Don't trust you, you see, not to tell somebody. We never were going to give you any money at all; not fifty dollars or a hundred. We had it in mind all along to kill you, just as soon as we'd got the information out of you.'

Thomas Jackson's heart was pounding thunderously with such force that he felt as though it might burst out of his chest. Then, just as he had reached that high pitch of terror from which he would never descend, Quinnell gave a slight nod. Another of the men came up softly behind Jackson and slipped a thin piece of rope around his neck. This was then

11

jerked tight as the trooper was strangled. In the final extremity of his agony, the dying man fouled himself, causing those murdering him to make loud and callous comments about the stink.

When he was dead, the corpse was pushed into a corner of the barn and covered with an old tarp, to be disposed of later.

As the sun rose on the day following Thomas Jackson's death Colonel Miguel Valentin de Lopez was pulling on his doeskin breeches and preparing to leave the Princess de Polignac's bedroom. From the bed that he had so recently vacated the princess appealed to him,

'Stay a little longer. Don't tell me you are sated?'

'For my own part I would be glad to linger,' replied the colonel, 'but I have an assignation which will not be denied.'

The woman laughed. 'What, another assignation? What is her name?'

'I am meeting His Majesty the Emperor in a little over an hour. It would be neither courteous nor wise to keep him waiting.'

'That absurd little man! How it must irk you to serve under such a simpleton.'

Colonel Lopez was not to be drawn into criticising his commander; he merely observed:

'He is not the worst man I have served.'

As he headed back to his quarters to wash and shave before his audience with Emperor Maximilian, Lopez reflected upon the strangeness of the fate that had ended with his being commanded by such a man as this.

Colonel Lopez was, at the age of forty, something of a legend in the Mexican army. He had conducted confidential and delicate business for four previous heads of state and all had found him to be the most useful man in their administrations. For the colonel got things done. He moved in 'mysterious ways his wonders to perform', as the hymn has it, achieving all manner of marvels and handling every assignment with unmatched discretion.

Being such a man as he was, it was no surprise that he already knew what the Emperor required of him. Indeed, he had guessed what his next task would be even before Maximilian himself had thought to send for him. Of course, something needed to be done about the flow of arms to the rebels in the north of the country: weapons that were being smuggled across the border from the United States. If the rifles could be prevented from crossing the Rio Grande from Texas, then the rebels would have only pitchforks and scythes to wield in their struggle with the army.

As it was, some units of the forces supporting former President Juarez were better equipped than his own men, with the latest repeating rifles; an intolerable situation that badly needed to be tackled. If, that was, the rebels were not to be successful in their efforts to drive out the French and install Benito Juarez as president once more.

The interview that Colonel Lopez had with his

Emperor was brief and to the point.

'I am told that you are a man who works miracles, Colonel. Is it so?' Maximilian asked.

'I have been fortunate enough to find my name connected with some praise in the past, Sire,' Lopez replied modestly.

'Yes, I apprehend that you were on the staff of that rascal Juarez. Before, that is, he was run out of the capital and into hiding. I believe they called him the "Dwarf Butcher", because of his bloodthirsty way with captured enemies. Is it not so?'

'I never heard that it was, Sire,' said Colonel Lopez, 'I only ever heard him referred to as "Excellency".'

'Well well, this is nothing to the purpose. Are you capable of cutting off the weapons to that deluded rabble who follow Juarez? Do so and I will promote you to General on your return.'

So it was that Colonel Miguel Valentin de Lopez embarked upon the most important mission of his career; one that would change his life for ever.

After Lee's surrender at Appomattox Court House on 9 April 1865 there were those in the Confederate Army who refused to put down their weapons and accept that the war was over. Such men were variously known as 'Diehards' or 'Holdfasts'. Units of the defeated army continued to harry the Federal forces for some months after the official surrender; generally by means of guerilla tactics.

Captain Barnabas Quinnell had been in command

of a group of guerillas in the closing days of the war and he saw no reason to stop fighting just because some of the senior officers felt minded to treat with the enemy. Quinnell and his men entertained a burning and abiding hatred for the Yankees and carried on ambushing their patrols and raiding their camps well into the summer.

By late June it was plain enough, even to men like Quinnell, that the South was thoroughly and comprehensively defeated and that the Yankees were in iron control of their lands. None of the men fighting with Quinnell had anything in particular to draw them back to their homes. The army had been their life for over four years now and the idea of taking the 'Ironclad Oath' and settling down to grub a living from dirt farming was not an attractive one.

So it was that the band of guerillas found itself transmuted, in the easiest way imaginable, into a band of bushwhackers. They still hit the Yankees, but from early July onwards all their activities had a strong business end in view. They seized a railroad depot in Louisiana, robbed the train of some silver it was carrying and massacred a platoon of Federal soldiers who stumbled into the station at the wrong time.

There were other attacks until the army began to hunt in earnest for Quinnell and his men, forcing the bushwhackers to move west into Texas. It was there that they heard of an opportunity to settle down and become legitimate soldiers once again.

Emperor Maximilian was currently being supported not only by his own army, but also by the

French troops who had put him on the throne on the first place. There were rumours, though, that Napoleon III was about to buckle to pressure from Washington and withdraw his forces, taking them home to France. Maximilian knew that his own army might not prove strong or loyal enough to defeat the uprising in the north of the country: a rebellion that centred around former President Benito Juarez. He needed extra men, men who would be loyal to him rather than to any patriotic notions about the Mexican nation.

In short, he was recruiting mercenaries who would destroy the rebels and reassert imperial authority in the north of Mexico. In return for the help of such men the Emperor was offering grants of land in a part of the country to be called 'New Virginia', as well as regular pay while they fought on his behalf.

Before they crossed the Rio Grande into Mexico and took up arms in the service of Emperor Maximilian, Quinnell's band were planning to carry out one final exploit: a little matter of theft and gun-running that would bring in enough cash to tide them over until they were able to start drawing a soldier's pay once more. The fact that this last piece of banditry was flatly opposed to the interests of the man who would soon be their patron, bothered them not in the slightest.

It was a modest enough enterprise that Captain Quinnell and his men planned to undertake before settling in Mexico and becoming soldiers of the

Emperor. They proposed to ambush a cavalry unit that was transporting some rifles from their base to an arsenal in New Mexico. Having acquired the weapons, Quinnell's men would sell them to the Mexican rebels, who were desperate for modern guns. Quinnell was not greedy; they would sell the rifles to Juarez's men for five dollars each and throw in the ammunition for free. This would net them a total of a little under $2,000, which should keep them in liquor and women until they could draw regular pay in their usual occupation.

On his journey up to the border Lopez reaped the benefits of a scheme which he had himself set up in 1862. There was at that time not a single yard of rail-road operating in the whole of Mexico. Ten years earlier Don Antonio Escandon had secured the franchise to build a railroad from Vera Cruz to Mexico City, but political upheavals had put paid to that scheme. In 1864, the project had been revived under a new company, the Imperial Mexican Railway Company, but there was still no track for a locomotive to run along.

Before Colonel Lopez took a hand in matters this had meant that travelling from one end of Mexico to the other was an arduous and time-consuming busi-ness. Even sending an order from the capital to some remote army garrison could take weeks. Not only was there no railroad, there were no telegraph lines either.

Lopez had suggested a system similar in many

ways to the late American Pony Express, with fresh horses being kept ready for government messengers every twenty miles or so along the main highways running north and east from Mexico City. This meant that when Colonel Lopez and his faithful sergeant set out for the American border on the morning of 7 August, they knew that the journey would take five days instead of fourteen or fifteen.

CHAPTER 2

Collecting the rifles, passing them to the rebels and then getting paid for them would take Quinnell and his boys about a week in total. They planned to be heading to Mexico City to sign up and fight for Maximilian by the end of August.

The eleven men were sprawling at their ease on a hill overlooking the narrow defile through which the road ran to New Mexico. Nearby was the little white-painted mission station of San Angelo.

'You think as that craven dog Jackson was giving a true bill when he said there'd only be six men in the escort?'

Quinnell considered the question carefully before answering. At length, he said:

'I can't say what reason he'd have for lying about it. I don't think as he'd've misled us, on account of he knew we'd come looking for him if he sold us a pup. No, I'd say that if he said six, then six it'll be.'

Lucid and plain expositions of this sort were what had persuaded the other ten men to continue accepting the captain as their leader after the war had ended. Barnabas Quinnell trusted nobody, regarding all men as born liars. He always started from this basic premise, and so none of his plans was dependent upon the good will of others, nor did they hinge upon trusting any persons other than his own men. It was a philosophy that had served him and the others well enough for the last four months.

'How do we play it, Captain?' asked Bob Wheeler, who had been a sergeant when they were all a bona fide military unit. 'We don't want to be hazarding our lives for two hundred dollars apiece.'

'You got that right, Bob my boy,' said Quinnell. 'I hope and pray that we'll all of us be able to cross the Rio Grande a week or so from now, and take up that emperor's kind offer of land to settle on and a job of soldiering to go along of it.'

'I'm a-wonderin' where we're going to be able to get clear with four hundred rifles and a ton of cartridges for the same,' said another man. 'Army'll be out with a view to huntin' down those guns, you can depend on it.'

'Been thinking the selfsame thing,' observed another. 'That wagon'll leave a good clear trail, bein' that heavy-laden. We not careful, we goin' to have the cavalry riding down on us and like as not hanging us on the spot.'

'These are good questions,' said Captain Quinnell, 'so I may as well tell you what I have in mind and you fellows can reason it out with me. First off is where we're not taking the cart away with us. We're going to burn it.'

The other men looked puzzled and uncertain.

'Come for a little walk and I'll show you what I want to do,' Quinnell went on.

He stood up; the rest of the group also got to their feet and followed their leader down the side of the hill in the direction of the ravine through which the road passed. By the time they were scrambling down the scree-covered slope to the roadway not one of them had worked out what their boss had in mind. Quinnell pointed south.

'Along come the wagons,' he said. 'We're ten miles from the base here, and it's another ten to Las Cruces, where they're going to be depositing them. All with me so far?'

There were nods and grunts of agreement. The captain continued:

'Well, we kill them all. I'll talk that over in a minute, but let's just say as they're all dead. We pick up a few rifles each and then carry them along on foot to here.' Matching the words to his actions he went through a pantomime performance of a man labouring under a heavy load as he stumped away from the road to the steeply sloping limestone sides of the defile. Lean thorn bushes grew here and there on the slopes, which stretched up at an angle of perhaps forty-five degrees. When he had reached the end of the level ground across which the road ran, Quinnell asked:

'Anybody notice anything?'

'Like what?' said Bob Wheeler, thoroughly perplexed by the captain's antics and unable to see what his boss was driving at.

Quinnell was grinning broadly as he bent down and rolled away a half-dozen small boulders. Then he pulled away a clump of thorn bushes to reveal a black hole, perhaps three feet deep and six feet long.

'What d'you say, boys?' he asked triumphantly.

'What is it?'

'Why, you slowpoke!' said the captain. 'It's a cave, of course. Goes right back into the hillside. Once you crawl in there it opens out a bit into a kind of tunnel. Unless you're right on top of it you'd never know it was there.'

Realization dawned in Bob Wheeler's eyes.

'So one of us crawls in there, I guess, and after the Yankees have all been killed we pass him the guns and ammunition. Cover up the hole and then torch the wagon. Then we sweep away any tracks near here and climb back up the slope to where we left our mounts. Those damn' Yankees will come up here, take away their dead and be altogether foxed as to how their guns was spirited away.'

Quinnell looked at his one-time sergeant with real affection.

'You have the whole thing measured and weighed,' he said. 'That's just exactly what I had thought of. What d'you say, Bob? Think it'll work?'

'I'd say that two hundred dollars apiece is as good as in our pockets. I suppose we just wait 'til they

Yankees have taken away their fallen comrades and suchlike, and then come up here with a wagon to collect the weaponry? What'll they think? That Mexes have spirited the guns away?'

The secret of Colonel Lopez's phenomenal success in his clandestine work for the government of Mexico was absurdly simple. There was at that time in the country a direct correlation between the degree to which a man looked European and his likelihood of advancement. The situation was not as bad as it was in the United States, where the idea of an Indian president, or even an Indian senator or congressman would have been unthinkable. In Mexico, Benito Juarez, a full-blooded Zapotec peasant, had become president in 1861, before being driven from the capital by the invading French forces. There were native Mexican army officers, politicians, doctors and lawyers, none of whom could have been in such positions across the Rio Grande in America.

Successful Mexicans were, however, very much the exceptions. To get on in Mexico most men concealed their native ancestry and claimed to be as Spanish as was feasible, given their appearance. The ruling elite were Spanish and so it was to this class that everybody aspired to belong.

Lopez was different. He made no attempt to hide his origins; like Juarez, his family were native Mexican peasants. Growing up, he had spoken Nahuatl, the commonest of the indigenous languages. This, combined with his obviously Mexican features, meant that Lopez had only to change into the ragged garb of a dirt farmer to be able to fit in among the ordinary people of Mexico and find out what they were thinking and feeling; something impossible for anyone whose native language and ancestry were Spanish.

The only concession that the colonel made to the expectations of the society in which he moved was to use his baptismal name, rather than the native one he had been given at birth. That was no shame though; even President Juarez was known by his Spanish and not his *Nahuatl* name.

By changing horses every twenty miles Colonel Lopez and Sergeant Carlos maintained a brisk pace. For much of the time they cantered, and then alternated this with periods of trotting to give their mounts a little rest. While they trotted side by side the two men conversed in an easy and familiar fashion.

'Tell me, sir,' said Carlos, 'are we really to stop this traffic in guns?'

'What else? You know what my orders are from his Imperial Majesty.'

Sergeant Carlos was too discreet a man to speak openly against the Emperor, limiting himself to remarking:

'They say that the French are already preparing to leave. I wonder how long our Emperor will last without their help?'

'All things are with God,' said Colonel Lopez

piously. 'Take care that your tongue does not run away with you, Carlos. Our Maximilian has long ears.'

Their conversation was conducted in the dialect of *Nahuatl* that was commonly spoken in the north of the country, up by El Paso. It would have taken a remarkable spy, possessed of godlike powers, to eavesdrop and then translate the muttered words of Sergeant Carlos. Nevertheless, the sergeant accepted the reproof of his superior without comment. They had never discussed the matter, but Carlos was fairly sure that he knew where the colonel's sympathies lay. He thought it politic, though, to leave that subject and move on to the practical details of the mission upon which they were engaged.

'Will we be taking some men from the garrison at Cueda when we cross the great river?' he asked.

'I will ask for volunteers. Twelve men should be enough for our purpose.'

'Volunteers? How so?'

'We cannot cross the border in uniform. It would give the Yankees the excuse to move into our country. I don't want to see American soldiers here, any more than I wish to see. . . .' Colonel Lopez did not complete the sentence, but it was plain that he meant to say: any more than I want the French here. Sergeant Carlos understood perfectly.

'So we will be going in civilian garb,' he said, 'and running the risk of being hanged as spies or murderers if we are caught?'

'That is so. What of you, Carlos? You are not afraid

to come with me?'

'I would follow you to hell, my Colonel.'

'Tush man, that will hardly be necessary,' said Lopez lightly. 'Just a few miles into the United States will be sufficient.'

When Captain Quinnell and his unit broke away from the army after the surrender in order to continue prosecuting the war against the Yankee invaders, they took with them all the equipment upon which they were able to lay their hands. As they saw it, all the weaponry would be handed over to the Federal forces as part of the terms of the peace, so they were robbing not the Confederacy but the Union Army by making off with the guns, along with the powder and shot for them. They had buried some of their haul, sealed in tarred paper and ready to dig up again when the time was right.

When they felt that it was an auspicious moment to leave Louisiana, the men had bought a wagon and loaded it up with all the weapons that they had taken from the arsenal at Baton Rouge. It was a considerable risk, for if they had been stopped by a Yankee patrol they were running the risk of being hanged out of hand. However, their luck held and they managed to bring the guns all the way across Texas and to unload them at a little farmhouse that they had rented just inside the New Mexico Territory.

Among the guns that Quinnell's men had at their disposal were three British-made Whitworth rifles. These were snipers' weapons, which could be sighted up to 1,200 yards. All three of these rifles were fitted with telescopic sights.

That the Whitworth was accurate at that range had been amply demonstrated by Bob Wheeler when he and Captain Quinnell had chanced to find themselves in Virginia and involved, in an informal capacity, in the battle for Spotsylvania Court House. Bob Wheeler was sporting a Whitworth at the time; he and the captain were en route south, to team up with the rest of the unit. They had halted at Spotsylvania because a siege was developing and they thought that they might be able to contribute something to it. In the event, Wheeler's role in the battle surpassed all expectation.

The Union forces were hunkered down, waiting for the assault to come. Some of what happened that day Wheeler and his friends only learned later. Wheeler could see that the Confederates were firing more or less at random towards the Federal position, just to make sure that the opposing side kept their heads down and didn't have much chance to look around and see what was happening.

The officer in overall command of the Union forces was a four-star general called John Sedgwick. He was, as they later heard, enormously irritated by the sight of his men lying down and crouching behind walls in case they got hit by stray shots from the snipers, who were firing pretty constantly towards them. The muskets being used by the Confederates were inaccurate at that distance and the minie balls just bounced around the buildings, hitting nobody.

When General Sedgwick came upon this scene he was amazed and appalled. He stood there, right out in the open and addressed his men thus:

'What's this I see? Men dodging around like this for single bullets? I'm ashamed of the lot of you! If you're like this with a few snipers, what will become of you when they open fire along the whole line?'

Of course, Segeant Wheeler couldn't have heard any of this, for he was crouched over a fallen tree trunk at a distance in excess of 1,000 yards. He was squinting along the narrow brass tube of the tele-scope that was mounted along the side of the Whitworth's barrel, unable to believe his luck in having in front of him the perfectly stationary target of a full general of the Union army. Sedgwick stood so still that he might have been posing to have his photograph taken in a studio.

General Sedgwick was getting into his stride now, ready to deliver a memorable tongue-lashing to the men lying in the dust around him.

'Yes, I'm plain ashamed of you,' he said. 'All else apart, those snipers couldn't hit an elephant at this distance!'

Whereupon, something over half a mile away, Bob Wheeler squeezed the trigger of his rifle and sent a large-calibre bullet speeding towards General Sedgwick. It was a perfect head-shot, taking him just below his left eye and causing the back of his head to disintegrate in gouts of blood, splinters of bone and

28

a spray of finely minced brain tissue.

Ever since that day Bob Wheeler had made sure that he always had a Whitworth near at hand. The disadvantages of the weapon – it was a muzzle-loader and heavier than the average piece – were vastly outweighed by its almost supernatural accuracy.

Captain Quinnell had told Wheeler, shortly after the murder of Trooper Jackson, that his ability with the Whitworth would be the key to their ambush of the Yankee soldiers and seizure of the rifles. Having reminded his old sergeant of this, Quinnell vanished for a couple of days, leaving the others to amuse themselves as best they were able in the remote little farmhouse that they had rented upon arriving in the state from Louisiana.

Two days before the Henry rifles were due to be moved up to the arsenal at Las Cruces, Captain Quinnell returned from his unexplained absence. Once he had dismounted the captain very carefully removed two stoneware bottles from his saddle-bag. One of the men asked:

'What's that you have? Moonshine?'

Quinnell laughed.

'Not hardly,' he replied softly. 'It's nitro.'

'You say what?' said the man, in a shocked voice, 'You mean it's nitroglycerin? God almighty! How much have you got there?'

'Two quart bottles, both full,' said Captain Quinnell imperturbably. 'A half-gallon in total. Five pounds in weight.'

'Shit! Five pounds o' nitro?' The man backed

away, a look of horror on his face.

Later, when the explosive had been safely cached in the barn, Quinnell set out the full plan for their little enterprise. The idea was simplicity itself. They would bury the bottles of nitroglycerin in the road, right in the path of the unit that would be transporting the rifles north. With only a half-dozen men riding escort, they would most likely not bother to put out flankers, but ride with four ahead of the wagon, the remaining two bringing up the rear. If Bob Wheeler could set off the nitro by firing at it just as the first riders were practically on top of it, then there was a good chance that all four troopers would be killed by the resulting explosion. The other men in Quinnell's band could then pick off the two riders at the back, along with whoever was driving the cart.

'You certain-sure that stuff is the real thing?' asked somebody.

'Where'd you get it, anyways?'

'They're doing some blasting at a quarry, over east,' said Quinnell. 'It's quicker work for them to use nitro. A sight better than black powder, at any rate. Ten times as powerful. Fellow there mixes it up as they need it.'

'It's going to take careful timing,' said Wheeler thoughtfully. 'We can't leave that stuff in the roadway overnight. We goin' to have to bury it just before the Yankees fetch up at the defile.'

'We've a clear view, almost as far as the base,' said the captain, 'when once we're perched on top of those rocks at the top of the pass at San Angelo. We've a good pair of field glasses. All it takes is to have a fellow on lookout duty, as'll tip us the wink when he sees them coming.'

'Even then, timing's going to be the key,' said Bob Wheeler once more. 'We don't want to blow up the wagon and destroy the rifles. Five pounds, you say? I'd think I should spring that mine when the riders are still six, maybe ten foot from it. They'll all be out of action for sure, and that way the wagon'll not be touched by the blast.'

'I'll leave it to you to judge that, Bob,' said Quinnell. 'You're the closest thing we have to a sapper, not to mention the best sniper I ever saw.'

A man who hadn't yet spoken asked a question that several of them had been pondering.

'If we're goin' to be fighting Juarez's guerrillas, you sure we goin' to want to make 'em a gift of these Henrys? They's sixteen-shooters, you know. More rapid firing than what we're like to be toting for our own selves.'

Captain Quinnell looked in approval at the man who had spoken.

'It's a good question,' he said. 'First off, of course, is where we're not making anybody a gift of these weapons. They'll be paying us five dollars a piece for them. But I was thinking the selfsame thing, that it kind of acts against our own best interests to be arming those rascally bandits.

'So what I thought was this. We wreck the bulk of them by smashing up the firing pins, but leave a few

31

good ones on top of the pile, just on the off-chance that they're minded to check one or two. That way we can maybe make it so as three hundred and fifty out of the four hundred are no use to man nor beast.'

There were chuckles of satisfaction upon hearing this proposal. The important thing was that they should all of them have a couple of hundred dollars to play with as they made their way south to New Virginia, the colony where they had been promised land.

'So we kill those bastards on the Saturday and hide the guns,' said somebody. 'They'll send out a search party from Las Cruces the same day, or I miss my guess. How long will we give them to lose interest in the place? Meaning, when do you think it'll be safe for us to collect the Henrys and make for the border?'

'We going to wait forty-eight hours,' said Quinnell firmly. 'During which time we don't go near nor by San Angelo and just sit tight here. We don't even go to Pike's Landing for those two days. It would be just our luck if those Union soldiers were sniffing round and came upon us. I don't want even the slightest chance of being recognized.'

So it was that the final plans were laid for the ambush that would pave the way for Barnabas Quinnell and his band of men to leave the United States and head off to settle in the heart of Mexico. As the saying goes, however: man proposeth, but God disposeth. While the former Confederates were setting their own ideas in motion, things were unfolding on the other side of the Rio Grande that would upset all their best-laid schemes.

CHAPTER 3

Three days before Captain Quinnell rejoined his band with a half-gallon of nitroglycerin in his possession, Colonel Lopez and his faithful sergeant rode over the crest of a hill and came upon such a scene as might have been found within the pages of Dante's *Inferno*.

One entire side of the hill over which Lopez and Carlos had just ridden had been cut away, leaving a bowl-shaped depression, hundreds of feet wide. Within this excavation scores of men and boys toiled, carrying baskets of earth from the depths of the pit and then emptying them some distance from it, creating, in the process, a range of miniature hills. Overseers on horseback rode back and forth, shouting at and cursing those undertaking the back-breaking work.

'Behold, our people!' said Sergeant Carlos, an unmistakable note of bitterness in his voice.

'What is this place?' asked Lopez, looking around in amazement. 'It was, for a certainty, not here the last time I travelled this road.'

'I would guess that they are following a vein of silver into the bowels of the earth,' replied Carlos. 'It is astonishing what you can achieve without machinery or explosives if only you have enough men with picks and shovels.'

'Some of those boys are no more than seven or eight years of age,' said Colonel Lopez indignantly. 'It is an outrage that they should be working so.'

Sergeant Carlos shrugged. 'What would you have? They are peons. They work to pay off debts incurred by their fathers, most likely.'

As the two uniformed men spoke together they reined in their horses without thinking. In a moment they were surrounded by boys who were unashamedly begging. They cried out in Spanish:

'*Por el amor de Dios, limosna, Excelencia!*' and '*Nos dan un poco!*': 'For the love of God, alms, Excellency, give us just a little!'

A sudden and uncontrollable fury erupted in Colonel Lopez's breast and for a moment he felt as though he would choke. It was obvious that these little ones had seen only the grand uniforms and had not even noticed that the men who wore them were native Mexicans like themselves.

He spoke fiercely, roused by the abject humility which these children displayed towards him:

'Have you no shame? Do you not see that I am one of you? Don't degrade yourselves!' He spoke in Nahuatl and the boys stared at him in amazement. They did not know what to make of one of their own people tricked out in such finery. Lopez continued:

'Have you no pride? Do you not know that the fathers of your fathers were Aztecs? They built mighty temples of worked stone when those Spanish dogs were still living in hovels.'

An expression of satisfaction came over Carlos's face as he heard this. His colonel was embarrassed at having spoken so and said to one of the boys:

'Come close to me. Have you honour?'

'I hope so.'

'See then, I give you this gold piece. It is not for you alone, I look to you to buy food for your friends and share it out equally. Will you do so?'

'I will.'

'Good boy.' Lopez turned to his sergeant and said, 'The day is wearing away. We must be off.'

That evening they found themselves within view of the Rio Grande. The garrison for which they were heading lay only a few miles away. It was at this point that the sergeant sprung a surprise, saying to Colonel Lopez:

'There is somebody who wished to meet you if you found yourself this far north.' Then he recollected himself and added, 'sir.'

'What's that? Whom do you speak of?'

'Will you trust me to conduct you to this person, sir?'

'I never yet knew you to mislead me, Carlos. If this is nothing contrary to my honour or the oaths I swore when I became a soldier, then you may take me to this person.'

'It is perhaps two hours' ride to the west.'

'Very well, lead the way.'

The flat, dusty land gradually gave way to a range of low rugged hills through which a narrow track wound its way. In truth, it would have been easier for the two men had they been riding mules up such trails, rather than their elegant horses.

'How do you know this part of the country?' asked Lopez after a while.

'I was born near here, sir. I received word some little time ago that a certain personage was staying in these hills.'

'I hope that I have not made an error in coming here.'

'I give you my word sir, that you have not.'

Twilight had fallen before they reached a little village of adobe dwellings.

'Wait here a moment, if you please,' Carlos said to his colonel. He dismounted and knocked on the door of one of the low, single-storey houses. After a minute or two he came out again and said:

'The man we want is in the last house.'

Colonel Lopez dismounted. He and Carlos led their horses along the single street of the village towards the very last house. It was somewhat larger than the other buildings, and as they approached it the two men could hear a hubbub of excited conversation, as though this building contained a noisy group of men all debating at the tops of their voices.

'Wait here for a moment, my Colonel,' said Sergeant Carlos. He knocked once at the door, then he vanished inside.

Waiting outside in the deepening gloom of the evening, Colonel Lopez was starting to wonder whether he had taken a wrong turn in accepting Carlos's mysterious invitation to meet with this 'personage'. Then the door opened, spilling yellow lamplight out into the gathering darkness.

A strange figure emerged, little taller than the eight- and nine-year-old boys who had been begging from Lopez at the silver mine. Almost without thinking the colonel bowed low and said,

'Your Excellency.'

Although it was no longer correct, strictly speaking, to address the former President of Mexico in this style, there was something about the presence of Benito Juarez that commanded respect, making a simple 'sir' sound hopelessly inadequate.

The day of the projected ambush dawned bright and clear. All the men were up before the sun had even peeped over the hills that lay to the east of their temporary home. It was essential for the success of their plan that Captain Quinnell and his men were all well concealed in and around San Angelo long before the Yankees arrived.

The defile was a perfect spot for an ambush and it was not in reason to suppose that the detachment of cavalry would be unaware of this, nor that they would neglect to scan the area for possible hazards as they approached. The war had ended so recently that without doubt such routine precautions as examining the high ground surrounding a narrow pass with field glasses before passing through, would still be observed as a matter of course.

Although none of the men had yet remarked upon it, for fear of appearing cowardly or nervous, the focus of every man's attention was on those two stoneware bottles of nitroglycerin.

Nitrogyclerin is a horridly sensitive and unpredictable substance. It is an oily liquid, produced by mixing together nitric and sulphuric acids in precise proportions and then adding a certain quantity of glycerin. The result is a high explosive which may be detonated by something as trivial as a sharp rap.

The liquid becomes more stable if absorbed by cotton waste to produce guncotton, or it can be decanted on to certain porous clays, which will soak it up and render it less likely to explode accidentally.

In the original form, though, there are few more hazardous substances; dropping one of those bottles or even banging one against the other could have spelt grievous injury or death for them all.

Captain Quinnell, fortunately, was a man who knew what he was about; he made no false move with the deadly material, stowing it with the utmost care into his saddle-bag. After he had done so he turned to the other men and chaffed them, saying:

'What a bunch of old women you are! Had I not fought alongside you fellows I would suppose that you were afeard of a few gills of nitro.'

'Only a damned fool would ignore that peril,' growled one man. 'I seed one mishap with a gallon of nitro, one time. I hope never to see another.'

'Well, well,' said Quinnell. 'Happen you're right. In any case I shall ride a little apart from you men on the way up to San Angelo. That way, if there should be an unfortunate accident the consequences of it will fall upon my head alone.'

Bob Wheeler, whom nobody had ever known to be afraid of anything in this world, snorted at this and said in a slightly contemptuous tone of voice:

'I'll ride along o' you, Captain. I ain't 'fraid of a little drop of nitro.'

The rest of the men were evidently a mite shamed on hearing this, because as they rode up to the defile they all kept close to the captain, as if to demonstrate that they too did not really fear the effects of an explosion. As they rode along Wheeler said:

'We needs must dig the hole for those bottles before the cavalry come into sight. I know as we don't want to be leaving 'em there for hours, in case a chance rider should pass through, but nor either do we want to be digging and burying 'em in a hurry.'

'I thought on this too,' said Quinnell. 'I was going to suggest the same thing but, as usual, you're a step ahead of me, Bob.'

'We'll need to work fast when we're a-buryin' of those rifles, too. There's a single cavalry trooper proceeds along that track between Las Cruces and the base at odd times. It would be unfortunate if one such saw what we was about.'

'I guess one more death wouldn't matter overmuch

between friends, hey?'

'I ain't fussed about the killin' of an extra Yankee. I'm also thinkin' about the devil of a noise that five pounds' weight o' nitro makes when it blows. It's apt to invite interest from those hereabouts. I know this is bare enough terrain, but you know what it's like. Some fool might come askin' questions.'

'You're a worrier, Bob,' said Captain Quinnell good-naturedly, 'that's what makes you so good at what we do. Don't fret now, we'll tell everybody to work as quick as they may when once we've killed those soldiers.'

The pass at San Angelo was a gap between a range of rocky hills that were too low really to be described as mountains. On the other hand they were too steep and rugged for a road to pass over, so the early pioneers had found a slight gap just wide enough for a wagon to pass through. The floor of this natural defile had been cleared of boulders and smoothed a little and now the road north to Las Cruces ran through it.

Hardly had he begun digging the hole in which the bottles of nitroglycerin would be concealed than Bob Wheeler ran into a slight problem. There had been a shower of rain the day before: no common event in this region during the summer months. It had moistened the ground, but the sun had dried out the top layer of dusty soil. Digging the hole, though, revealed the darker damp earth, and this showed starkly against the paler, dry soil that covered the surface of the road.

41

It took a considerable time to scoop out the darker material and carry it right away from the road so that it would not be noticed. The last thing they needed to end up with was a prominent, dark, circular patch set right in the middle of the roadway. Even the blindest trooper would spot it and wonder what was amiss.

Arranging this to Bob Wheeler's satisfaction took some time; he made a pile of dry topsoil near the hole so that this could be scattered over it when the bottles had been put in place. By the time that everything was ready the sun was pretty high in the sky and Captain Quinnell's gold hunter told him that it lacked only five minutes to half past nine. A man was scanning the horizon anxiously with field glasses, keeping a watch for the cavalry unit.

The men who were not actually digging the hole or doing anything else of any use were lying in various hollows among the rocks, taking their ease. They could not even smoke, as the fanatically careful Wheeler was worried that some wisp of smoke might be seen by the cavalry as they drew close. At length there came a cry from the lookout:

'They's a comin'!'

At precisely the moment when Jack Cartwright was hollering out that the cavalry were coming, Colonel Miguel Valentin de Lopez was standing on the sentry walk of the wall of a little fort overlooking the Rio Grande River at Cueda. He was brooding about his interview, five days earlier, with President Juarez. Or rather, as he corrected himself irritably, former President Juarez.

When he had realized precisely who it was that Sergeant Carlos had brought him to meet Lopez expected the former president to beg him not to disrupt the arms smuggling that was taking place across the border. This would have been embarrassing, because Lopez had his orders direct from the head of state and had no intention of deviating from them. He had agreed to strike at the gunrunners and that was what he proposed to do. But it had been for quite a different purpose that Juarez had wished to see him.

Benito Juarez was the shortest grown man that Lopez had ever met in the whole course of his life. He was only four feet six inches tall; had he lacked but another few inches he might have passed as a circus midget or carnival sideshow freak. It was for this reason, combined with his utter ruthlessness, that Juarez had indeed been known by his enemies as the 'Dwarf Butcher', though Colonel Lopez had denied any knowledge of this nickname.

What he lacked in physical size, however, Juarez made up for in dignity and personal magnetism. He radiated power and confidence. Lopez had read that the first Napoleon, uncle of the present French emperor, had combined a small stature with great force of personality in much the same way.

The last President of Mexico had greeted Lopez with the greatest affability and condescension.

'You look well, Colonel. I hear that you are even

more in favour than was the case when I last availed myself of your services. You have the happy knack of pleasing any leader.'

'Your Excellency is most kind.'

'You are here to deal with the gunrunners, I think? Ah, you are discreet and will not confirm it to be so. That is all very right and proper. And now you think that I shall put you in a damnable position by asking that you go easily on such men, no?'

Since that had been exactly what Colonel Lopez had thought he said nothing, wondering what would follow.

'I will confide in you, Colonel Lopez,' Juarez continued: 'We are soon to be supplied by the Americans themselves. They wish to be rid of European influence on this continent and feel that giving us the necessary tools will save them from going to all the trouble of invading Mexico. There, what do you say to that?'

There had been little that Lopez could say, so he had remained silent. It made perfect sense as soon as Juarez told him and he knew at once that what the president – former president – said was perfectly true.

'You wonder why I asked that you be brought here to see me, Colonel, is that so?'

Lopez had shrugged.

'I will tell you. I have a warning for you and also an offer. You are in no danger, even if you refuse the offer, but it as well that you know what that "emperor" is about, because it means the end of the country that you and I both love.'

Then, standing there in that little street in the tiny village, Juarez had outlined the plan that the Emperor Maximilian had devised to preserve his tenuous hold upon the throne. It was indeed a scheme that would spell the end of the country in which Lopez had grown up. After that came the offer, which was, as the colonel had guessed all along, that of a job as leader of Juarez's troops in the revolution which, he believed, was about to topple the foreign ruler.

Sergeant Carlos came up the ladder and walked along the sentry walk to where his master stood brooding.

'Do you wish, sir, to cross the river this morning or shall we wait until dark?' he asked. While they were at a military base Carlos was most punctilious about using the correct forms of military address. Lopez looked at the man curiously and said quietly:

'Before we left the Emperor offered to promote me to general if our mission here should be successful. You understand what that means?'

'It means that he is minded to place you in command of his whole army, I guess.'

'If I rose to such heights, you could come with me. Why, you could become an officer yourself. How would that be?'

Carlos looked at him inscrutably.

'You will do as best suits your purposes, sir,' he replied.

'It might suit your purposes too, Sergeant.'

'How so? To see our people ground down like the Negro slaves who until a few short months ago were traded like cattle, not far from here?'

'Keep your voice low, man. You don't want everybody to know how you feel. Tell me, would you come with me if I asked, and still be my helper? If I became a general, I mean.'

'We must survive the next week first, sir,' said Sergeant Carlos carefully. 'Is it not said that you should not count your eggs until they are in the basket?'

'Even so is it said.'

That morning the ten men who had volunteered for the special mission across the border changed into the typical clothing of Mexican peasants of the peon class: rough, bleached linen tunics and trousers. They would be taking weapons with them, but these they would not wear openly, not once they were across the border. The sight of rough working men such as they appeared to be, going about armed, would invite too many questions from the Anglos.

The men who were to accompany Colonel Lopez and Sergeant Carlos across the border and into the United States had volunteered for the mission for two reasons. In the first instance, life in the fort was so monotonous and dull as could hardly be imagined. At least this way they would be able to live a little. The second incentive was that each man thought that he might be able to distinguish himself in some way in front of the renowned Colonel

Lopez. Such adventures led sometimes to medals and also to sudden promotion.

The fact that if captured by the American army they would be liable to summary execution as spies did not seem to weigh very heavily in the balance. It was well known that the Yankees could not tell one peasant from another and they would be very unlikely to identify one of them as being a serving soldier in the Imperial army.

So it was that the twelve men, all dressed in their nondescript clothing, set out across the Rio Grande in two well-provisioned rowing boats. Their aim, as Lopez had explained to them before they began their journey, was to strike fear into the hearts of any man who thought that there might be a profit in running guns to the rebels.

He did not think it necessary to mention that, from all that he now apprehended after talking to the former president, their actions would make not the slightest difference to the situation. If what Juarez had said was true the Americans were already getting ready to bring large consignments of weaponry of all kinds down to El Paso, where it would conveniently be 'lost'.

So it was that Colonel Lopez was able to undertake with perfect fidelity the mission that he had promised to perform for the Emperor in Mexico City, while at the same time not working in any degree against the best interests of the Mexican people.

47

CHAPTER 4

The column of dust kicked up by the oncoming wagon and its escort hung like a pall of grey smoke in the morning air. Quinnell and Bob Wheeler made their way down the slope towards the hole that had been dug to receive the stoneware flasks. The other men positioned themselves so that they were quite out of sight of the men heading their way. There were four men positioned on either side of the rocks overlooking the road; their intention was to maintain a flanking fire, killing every member of the detachment as soon as possible after the nitroglycerin had been detonated.

In addition to Wheeler, carrying a Whitworth that he would use to set off the charge, two of the other men were also armed with the same type of weapon. It would be their job to take out the driver of the wagon, along with anybody else who survived the explosion. Those without Whitworths would just throw as much lead down into the defile as they could. It was of course absolutely vital that none of the troopers should escape and ride to Las Cruces to raise the alarm.

Even Wheeler, whose nerves were all but unde-tectable, felt a little uneasy at the speed with which Captain Quinnell sprinted down the slope, carrying the bottles of nitro one in either hand. It would take only the slightest slip of a foot and there would be no putting matters right in this world. By God's grace they gained the floor of the little valley without any mishap and the captain placed the two bottles care-fully into the hole that they had earlier excavated.

Although they were in a great hurry neither Quinnell nor Wheeler flung handfuls of dirt and stones unthinkingly into the hole containing the explosives. Instead, they very carefully packed damp soil around the bottles and then sprinkled dry earth around them, leaving only the corks visible above the surface of the roadway.

'You have enough to aim at?' asked Quinnell.

'The size of ball I'm using, it'll be 'nuff if'n I just hit near by,' replied Wheeler. 'Don't fret, I ain't about to miss.'

'Never thought it for a moment.'

The two men scrambled back up the rocks to join the others on that side of the ravine. Five pounds of nitro makes a pretty sizeable explosion and they had all been sure to take up positions that would be far enough from the roadway to make it unlikely that they would be injured by any stones sent in their direction when Bob Wheeler fired. None of the others would, in any case, be showing themselves above the rocks until the mines had been detonated. Only one man's head needed to be peering down into the valley: that of the one who was actually going to trigger the massacre.

Everybody kept utterly still and quiet as the rattle of the wagon and the steady drumming of the horses' hoofs could be heard more and more clearly. Only Bob Wheeler could actually see the little group of riders surrounding the wagon that they were guarding.

Even so, he could only just see them from the corner of his eye; he certainly had no intention of turning his head to the left to see the formation with greater clarity. He had seen operations spoiled in that way, when some alert hostile caught the faintest glimpse of movement up ahead and then the enemy troop scattered and took cover. All Wheeler's attention was focused upon the tiny dot in the road below that indicated where the bottles of nitroglycerin had been buried.

It was a matter of the finest judgement. A fraction of a second too soon and only the front two riders might be incapacitated by the blast; a moment too late and the wagon itself and its precious load might be fearfully damaged. Through the telescope Wheeler could see the cross hairs centred a little in front of the corks. With his left eye he was aware of the little cavalcade coming ever closer.

He gauged that the lead riders were ten feet or so in front of the corks when he took a deep breath, held it for a heartbeat and then squeezed the trigger.

The results of the shot surpassed all expectations. The roadway in front of the horses blew up like a volcano, killing the leading horses and their riders instantly. As he and Quinnell had anticipated, there were four riders leading the wagon and two trailing a little way behind it.

Before the echo of the blast had had time to travel back and forth between the rock-strewn slopes that lined the defile, Quinnell's other men opened up on the survivors, every one of whom was killed in the first round of firing. Although as soon as he had set off the explosives Wheeler had reloaded as swiftly as he was able, by the time he had done so and was sighting once again along the thin brass tube of the telescope there were no living targets at which to aim. Two of the horses seemed to be uninjured, but that was all. Every one of the seven men who had entered the ravine a few seconds earlier now lay dead.

Without delay the whole band of Quinnell's men went scooting down the slopes to the road. The captain shouted as they ran down:

'Cartwright, get yourself in that cave and be ready to stack the rifles and ammunition. And take their side arms too, carbines and pistols. I dare say we can use them.'

'Aye aye, Captain!' Cartwright shouted back face-tiously. They were all of them laughing gaily, relieved that the ambush had gone so smoothly with no losses to their own side.

It took half an hour to hide the armaments in the

cramped cave and another ten minutes to disguise the opening with rocks and plants. There was no earthly reason to suppose that the Yankees, when they came, would be hunting for any hiding-place. Most likely they would assume that the raiders had carried off the guns, somehow concealing their tracks very well.

Once everything was done they took a couple of thorny branches and swept the tracks away from the entrance to the cave. Then they did the same around the wagon. When this had been done all the men except Bob Wheeler retreated up the slopes to where their horses had been tethered out of sight. Wheeler took a small flask of lamp oil from inside his jacket and sprinkled it liberally over the wagon. Then he struck a lucifer and dropped it on the oil, which immediately flared up. Wheeler backed away quickly, brushing away his own tracks until he reached the rising rocky ground. Then he darted off the road and dashed up the slope.

The wagon was blazing merrily, sending up clouds of grey-blue wood smoke. The two parties led their horses down through the hills until they reached level ground again. Then they trotted off along the road, their tracks mingling with those made earlier by the cavalry unit. When men were sent out from Las Cruces, probably later that same day, they would have a pretty riddle to read! Perhaps they would assume that native Mexicans were responsible for the murder of the troopers and the theft of the rifles.

One thing was for sure: they would be most unlikely to find the guns where they had been hidden by the side of the road. In forty-eight hours Quuinnell's men could collect them and then make for the Rio Grande and their new life as soldiers of the Emperor Maximilian.

Once Colonel Lopez and his eleven companions landed on the far shore of the river they became, in effect, spies: soldiers masquerading as civilians. By all the rules and usage of war they would be liable to a drumhead court martial, followed by summary execution if found guilty.

Their first aim was to make their way to a little place on the edge of New Mexico, called Pike's Landing, where, it was rumoured, gunrunners were in the habit of meeting. Lopez and Carlos alone knew that this was a futile exercise and that, whatever action they took against the transport of arms across the border, weapons would soon be flooding into El Paso and then handed over wholesale to Juarez and his supporters.

The colonel's mind was torn between two impulses; he could not for the life of him decide which would prevail. He had promised Maximilian that he would come here and deal with the American gunrunners and that was just what he was doing. Having pledged his word he felt that, whatever else he decided to do in the future, he at least owed the Emperor this. After that? That was the question.

He was, it seemed, a man in great demand. The Emperor Maximilian had as good as assured him that he would be given the command of the Imperial army if he succeeded in this matter. Juarez too wanted him to lead the rebels who supported him. It was not often that a man was offered command of both sides in a war.

The thing tormenting Lopez most was the plan that Juarez had explained to him: the Emperor Maximilian's enterprise for ensuring that he remained on the throne for ever and handed the rule of this country down to his descendants throughout the ages. Even if he had not trusted the word of the former president and known him for an honourable man, the story he told made sense and fitted in with a number of things that the colonel himself had been hearing in recent months.

In short, the idea was to turn Mexico into a European colony, like the one that Britain had created in India. Maximilian had invited any defeated Confederates to come and live in his country, offering them, as an inducement, grants of land. These men would be so grateful that they might very well be prepared to fight for the Emperor against those who opposed his rule.

This area of colonization, lying between Mexico City and Vera Cruz, had been named New Virginia. There the Confederates would be able to live pretty much as they had done in the Southern states before the recent war. The Mexican peasants would be seen in the same light as the Negroes and would do all the backbreaking labour on the land.

More than this, Maximilian had apparently sent word to the countries of Europe, inviting emigrants to come to the country and begin 'civilizing' it. The aim was clear: to turn it into a nation of white Anglos like the United States. The native Mexicans would be worked to death on plantations, or herded into reservations just as the Indians were north of the Rio Grande. If he, Miguel Lopez, took up the Emperor's offer of promotion to general, then he would presumably be in command of the troops who would enforce such a detestable policy.

The more he turned the matter over in his mind the greater became Lopez's determination that such a fate should never befall his beloved country. The only question was: how best would he be able to thwart Maximilian's designs? By fighting against him on the side of the rebels or by commanding the Imperial army? He would need to come to a firm decision about this before the time came for him to return to Mexico City and accept his promotion.

Once the boats were beached it was a matter of some urgency to start marching north towards the New Mexico Territory. At first they endeavoured to conceal the dinghies. Each man had a pack, these were of varying sizes, shapes and colours. Anything in the least matching something else was to be avoided at all costs. In these packs were stowed short carbines that had had the barrel detached from the stock. In addition, each man had also a pistol, flask of powder, box of caps and a dozen paper cartridges for their carbines, a canteen of water and iron rations. On top of the packs every man had lashed an entrenching tool, short pick or spade. They looked just exactly like what they purported to be; that is to say, itinerant miners who had crossed over to the United States in search of work. When the men were all assembled with their packs on their backs Colonel Lopez addressed them.

'Men, we are heading north on a forced march. It will take us two days to reach the village for which we are heading. As some of you know, the Anglos are busying themselves in the affairs of our nation by smuggling arms across the border. We are to discourage them from this activity and perhaps make an example of one or two of them. Does anybody have any questions?'

Soldiers in the Imperial army of Mexico were not, in general, encouraged to query the orders of their superior officers, so nobody asked anything. Lopez had a few final words to say:

'I do not wish to see anybody marching in step or behaving in any way like a soldier. You may slouch along as you will, talk, smoke, spit and generally behave like a band of peons, lately escaped from servitude. Is this clear?'

It was clear and the men rejoiced to discover that they could relax a little. This expedition promised to make a very pleasant change indeed from endless drilling and guard duty that was the lot of the soldiers in the forts that lined the frontier.

*

Having wiped out the cavalry detachment and hidden the weapons that they had been after, it might perhaps have been thought that the members of Captain Quinnell's group would now be happy to relax and take it easy for a few days at the farmhouse where they were living. Unfortunately, men of that type are happy enough when they are in action, but if they have no external enemy it is all too often the case that, like caged animals, they will turn upon each other.

It was Quinnell's ruling that nobody should be seen outside the farmhouse for the forty-eight hours after the massacre at San Angelo. His reasoning was that the army might be sniffing around the area. If they came across an isolated house containing a dozen men it might invite enquiry.

So, apart from answering calls of nature, nobody left the farmhouse once they got back from their action. By the afternoon of the next day some of the men were getting restless and irritable. Maybe it was a mild form of cabin fever or some such, because these fellows were not really ones for reading and study. Indoor life did not suit them. There were one or two desultory games of poker to pass the time and it was in the course of one of these that the trouble flared.

The first anybody knew of it was when a shouted insult was heard from an upstairs room of the house. Most of the men were sitting in the kitchen, where there was a vast iron range and a plentiful supply of coffee. There came an angry yell from overhead:

57

'You lyin' cowson. You never did get that hand by fair play.'

There was a sound of scuffling, then a piece of furniture was evidently overturned. The captain got to his feet and said:

'I'll deal with it.'

It would have been quite natural and less alarming if, as Quinnell made his way up the stairs, he could have heard the sound of a fist fight in progress. But he did not. The only sound was of low voices, hissing in fury. He went to the room above the kitchen and found Jack Cartwright and another man who was universally known, for some reason, as 'Chips', standing facing each other, their faces white with anger.

'Now then,' said Quinnell cheerfully, 'what's all this about?'

'That bastard accused me of cheating,' said Chips. 'Claimed as I'd palmed a knave the hand before, and produced it to beat his pairs.'

Quinnell, who wasn't much of a one for playing at cards, said soothingly:

'Well, well. I dare say there's been some kind of mix-up. Why don't you fellows just shake and then come downstairs and have a coffee?'

'I'll see that whore's son in his grave,' Cartwright said,' 'fore I drink with him again.'

'Now there's no call for talk like that. . . .' began Quinnell, a little more firmly.

'See me in my grave, will you?' said Chips, in a low, dangerous voice. 'I'd like to see you lay me there, boy.'

'You would? Why then, ain't you the lucky one. You want to try conclusions with me? Fetch your iron and meet me out in the yard.'

Quinnell had the feeling that things were spiralling out of control.

'Nobody's going to start shooting outside,' he said sharply. 'Are you both quite mad? The army has patrols all over, looking for hide or hair of the men who killed those troopers. You'll bring them down on us like a duck on a June-bug. There'll be no shooting outside and attracting attention to the house in that way.'

'Then we'll fight in here,' said Jack Cartwright. ' 'Less'n this one's too yellow.'

'Yellow is it? You'll see who's yellow.'

Barnabas Quinnell had had a good deal of experience of life. He had owned a plantation before the war and had spent the last four years commanding men in various situations. He could see that these two young fools were absolutely determined to fight each other in mortal combat. It was a damned nuisance, but there was little he could do to prevent it. The most he could hope for was that their hotheaded antics did not cast the rest of the group in hazard and end with them being hanged for carrying out the attack at San Angelo.

'If you boys are sure you want to fight,' he said, 'then at least you can do it in here. That way you won't be risking our necks as well.' Even as he was speaking, Quinnell was wondering if he couldn't discourage the men from actually shooting at each other by making the circumstances of the duello such that it would be sure to result in death for one or both of them. It might bring them to their senses.

'You both best arm yourselves if you're fixed upon doing this,' Quinnell told the two youngsters. They went off, not looking one at the other, and a few minutes later returned, having buckled on their holsters. In the meantime the captain had fetched a silk cravat which he sometimes affected.

When the three of them were once more together in the upstairs room Quinnell tried one last time to stop the two men from fighting.

'Listen,' he said, 'you both showed that you're ready to fight. I reckon as that should be enough. Why don't the pair of you just shake hands now and call it a misunderstanding. I know you're friends in the usual way of things. What do you say?'

For a moment the matter rested on the edge of a razor. The two men looked into each other's eyes and it was clear that they were wavering. Then Jack Cartwright broke the spell:

'If'n he apologizes to me for sharpin' the cards,' he said, 'then I guess we can call it quits.'

'Sharpin'? Boy, you better be ready to back that up.'

'Enough,' said Quinnell, suddenly tiring of the folly of the business. He liked both young men and felt sure that this was no more than a silly misunderstanding. 'You're both right-handed? Then take this scarf in your right hands and face each other. You'll have to go for your pieces with your left hands. I'm going down those stairs and I'll count to three from the bottom of the staircase. On three you fire as best you can, without letting go of that cravat of mine. And mind you don't get it all bloodied up, I set a store by that thing.'

With great reluctance Captain Quinnell walked slowly down the stairs. When he reached the bottom, he called up, 'Can you boys hear me now?'

There were cries of assent and he sighed at the stubborness of youth. Those young fools were quite prepared to kill or be killed over this nonsense. The most stupid aspect of the whole affair was that the men hadn't even been playing for money. He had seen the slivers and chips of wood that they had been using. Quinnell shouted:

'One!'

The men in the kitchen were clustered in the doorway, peering out into the hall at the captain. He shook his head wearily, to indicate that he had no liking for the role in which he now found himself.

'Two!'

Most of the men in the house had either witnessed or indeed been party to this kind of thing. In nine cases out of ten nobody was killed in such contests. Just the firing of a few wildly aimed balls was sufficient to satisfy the honour of those participating in such affairs. This was slightly different, though. It was one thing to fire drunkenly at a man in the street from a distance of fifty feet or more. The two men upstairs were cold sober though, and in the same room; it would be sheer murder.

61

Captain Quinnell took a deep breath.

'Three!' he cried.

Immediately there came the crash of gunfire; first a single shot and then a veritable fusillade of fire. Following this there was dead silence. With heavy heart, the captain walked up the stairs and looked into the room. Through the thick smoke he could see that both men were lying on the bare boards. Their right hands were still entwined in his cravat, but the pair of them were stone dead. His cravat, he was pleased to observe, had not a mark upon it.

The others crowded into the room and gazed sadly at the lifeless bodies of their former comrades.

'What was it all about?' Bob Wheeler asked.

'Cartwright accused Chips of cheating at play. Said something about a knave turning up too soon, thought Chips had palmed it or something.'

Wheeler picked up the deck of cards and leafed through it curiously. It was of a standard design, with a vaguely geometric red pattern on the backs of the cards. Bob Wheeler laughed bitterly and said:

'You see what's happened here? Anybody know where they got this deck?'

'Found it in a drawer downstairs, I think,' said somebody.

'Well then, here's what's what. There's one complete deck here and a few cards from another pack. Same design on the back, but a mite older by the look of 'em. Look now, there's six knaves and five aces. Chips weren't cheatin', but it's easy enough to see how Jack Cartwright jumped to that conclusion.

62

'He must o' folded and seen the knave of hearts go on the bottom of the deck here and then, the very next hand, he sees Chips has the knave of hearts again. Must o' seemed like a right suspicious circumstance.'

'You mean,' asked another man, 'that it was all for nothing? They killed each other for naught?'

'That's the strength of it,' said Wheeler. 'It's the hell of a thing to happen.'

CHAPTER 5

Colonel Lopez and Sergeant Carlos marched a little apart from the other men so that they could engage in private conversation. Around half the soldiers from the fort were also native Mexicans and Lopez had no wish to be overheard and understood by these men. Weighty matters were at stake and he needed to make decisions on his own account, without fearing that others might involve themselves in his plans or offer unsolicited advice.

'How much do you know of these colonies?' Lopez asked the sergeant. Carlos hesitated for a moment before replying, as though he was unsure of the wisdom of revealing all that he knew.

'I know that foreigners are coming here at His Imperial Majesty's invitation. Also that they have been promised cheap workers for their land. Men, women and children who will work for years on the edge of starvation.' Carlos's voice rose with indignation and a couple of men near by turned to stare at him.

'Speak softer,' said the colonel, 'we need not make all the world and his dog a party to this. You know, then, that our former president believes that Mexicans like us will end up in the same case as those who live in this country? That the Anglos and their friends will rule Mexico?'

'One hears that not only Confederates are coming. They say that English are wishing to help our country develop as well.'

'You know, Carlos,' said Colonel Lopez, 'I think sometimes that you know more of this business than I do myself. Did you hear, then, that His Highness wishes to extend peonaje, until it encompasses almost all our people?' Although they were speaking in Nahuatl, Lopez used the Spanish word, there being no term in his own tongue to describe such an iniquitous system.

The *peons* of Mexico were at the very bottom of that country's social scale. A large number of them had been reduced to a status that differed little from slavery. Unscrupulous entrepreneurs would lend money to starving men so that they might feed their families in exchange for putting their mark on a contract. This was an agreement that they would work for some employer until the debt and all the interest that accrued had been paid off in full.

Since the majority of these poor people could not read or write the contracts meant nothing to them. This debt bondage, as it was sometimes known, could be assigned to another or sold on to another employer. If the man who had borrowed the money should happen to die, this did not release his family from the obligation. His children would then inherit the debt, which grew ever larger over the years as the interest was added to the capital sum owed by the wretched family. There was never any realistic hope of being free of the ever-accumulating debt.

In his conversation with Lopez the former president had told him that the foreign settlers would be encouraged to create more and more debt bondage, until most of the native Mexicans were caught in the trap and forced to work for no more than a meagre allowance of food. It would be the introduction of slavery in all but name.

Sergeant Carlos said: 'I am, like you, my Colonel, Mexican. So is Juarez. I trust his word.'

'I tell you this in truth,' Lopez went on, 'Benito Juarez is very far from being a saint. Not for nothing was he known as "The Butcher".'

'If I am to be oppressed and mistreated by those above me,' replied the practical and unsentimental sergeant, 'then I would rather suffer under a Mexican than an Austrian.'

'You speak truly. Let us finish this job for His Imperial Majesty and then see what chances. There is no purpose in going to meet trouble halfway. It arrives of its own accord soon enough.'

That evening Lopez and his men camped by a little tributary of the Pecos River. It was still twenty miles to Pike's Landing and they had managed so far to progress through the country without attacting any unfavourable attention. Lopez wished to be sure that the men were alert and ready for action when the need arose. After they had eaten, he spoke to them:

'We will have some weapons drill. On the word of command I would have you all assemble your carbines. Now, do so!'

There was a flurry of activity as the soldiers scrabbled in their packs for the tools necessary to attach the barrels and firing mechanisms to the stocks. It took a full quarter-hour before every man had his weapon ready and primed. Colonel Lopez did not stint in giving his opinion of this lamentable performance.

'I have been a soldier of the Mexican army since I was barely a child,' he told them, 'and never yet have I seen such a shocking display. Are you soldiers? Are you Mexicans?' He turned to Carlos.

'I am going for a stroll alone,' he said. 'I shall be gone perhaps half an hour. When I return I would see these men better organized.'

As Lopez left the camp he heard Carlos abusing the men, saying:

'*Ai*, you sons of dogs and low women! Is it so that you behave in front of the greatest officer in the army?'

When Colonel Lopez returned from his stroll Carlos had worked some magic upon the men; this time when the order was given to prepare their weapons they took only two minutes to have their carbines ready for use.

*

The deaths of Cartwright and Chips cast somewhat of a pall over the farmhouse. Both men had been well liked and the fact that they had died needlessly in such a pointless way had the effect of depressing the others.

'That Jack was a hasty fellow and no mistake,' remarked somebody. 'It could o' been any one of us as he took to accusing of cheating.'

'Isn't that the truth? Lordy, I'm right glad that it was Chips and not me that he fell out with! Still, I miss the two of them. It's what you might call a pointless death.'

Another man hawked and then spat in the fireplace.

'All deaths is pointless,' he observed, 'whether you're shot over gambling or on the battlefield, it amounts to the same thing. You're just as dead.'

Captain Quinnell came into the kitchen at this point.

'Let's not talk so much about death,' he said. 'It's not apt to be lucky. Listen, tomorrow evening we'll take a turn over to Pike's Landing and see what's to do. I reckon that the cavalry have had about long enough now to go sniffing about up at San Angelo. They've not been here and that means that, like as not, they've just taken off their dead and written off those rifles.'

'A drink or two in the saloon wouldn't come amiss,' said one man. 'You get kind of tired, bein''

68

cooped up like this with your friends. No offence to any o' the present company meant.'

By the following evening all the men apart from Quinnell and Wheeler were showing signs of irritation with their confinement; it was with a great feeling of relief that they trooped off in the direction of Pike's Landing. The day was sunny and bright, as one would expect in August and once they were free of the farmhouse the men cheered up considerably.

They had buried Cartwright and Chips at night, by the light of flaming pine torches. Nobody had had a Bible near at hand, so they'd simply stood for a minute in silence, offering their respects to the dead men.

The Lucky Lady saloon was virtually empty when they arrived and it didn't take long for their depression to vanish like the morning dew. Within an hour all of them were boisterous and gay. Or leastways, they were in that condition until two grubby-looking Mexicans came through the door. Their conversations stopped as they watched the two men walk uncertainly towards the bar. One was tall and had a kind of stateliness that was not commonly seen in Mexicans. The other was short and more homely-looking.

As the men passed by one of the tables at which some of Quinnell's men were sitting Bob Wheeler stuck out his foot and sent the shorter of the two men sprawling to the sawdust-covered floor. The others roared with laughter.

'You're a bit clumsy there, fella,' said Wheeler, a broad grin on his face. 'Need to set watch on how you're walkin'.' He winked at his friends.

The Mexican got to his feet and dusted off his clothing. He studiously ignored the man who had tripped him up and carried on walking to the bar. When he and his companion reached it the barkeep started polishing glasses with a dirty rag. He didn't even look at them, but muttered:

'Sorry. Can't serve you. It's the law.'

While the two Mexicans stood there, apparently undecided about what to do next, Bob Wheeler and two other men stood up and walked over to where they were standing.

'Christ, what's that stink?' Wheeler said. 'Eaugh! I never smelled the like.' He leaned closer to the men and then wrinkled his nose, saying:

'I thought as much. Why'nt you two get the hell out of here? You Mexes got places o' your own where you can stand. I guess you don't notice the stink if you're with the same breed.'

Both the men turned to face Wheeler. He noticed at once that they neither of them had that hangdog look about them that he expected to see in Mexicans. They met his eyes, staring boldly at him as though he were beneath them in some way. Their expressions infuriated Wheeler; grabbing them by the scruffs of their necks he began to hustle them out of the bar.

'You dirty heathens need to know who's on top,'

70

he said angrily as they neared the door. 'Come struttin' about in here, like you're as good as us!'

When they reached the door one of Wheeler's friends helpfully opened it for him and he thrust the Mexicans out into the street. The taller man seemed too slow to move and Wheeler gave him a kick up his behind, which knocked him over. Then Wheeler stood in the doorway for a moment, savouring his triumph, before turning and rejoining the others.

As the Mexicans walked thoughtfully along the single street that made up Pike's Landing, the shorter of the two said:

'That's how we will all be treated in our own country before long, if the Emperor has his way.'

'Those men are Confederates, or I am no judge of such things,' said Colonel Lopez. 'Without a doubt, we have come upon a nest of those very men whom I promised to deal with.'

Carlos smiled.

'It is seldom, my Colonel, that we as soldiers are able to combine pleasure with a strict attention to duty. It will be a joy to me to kill those Anglos.'

'Not so hasty. Let us be sure what they are about. I will not kill a man simply for kicking me in a certain part of my body. If they are gunrunners, then we shall by all means make an example of them.'

'They are sons of whores,' said Carlos confidently, 'and I feel in my bones that we shall come up against them again before much longer.'

'It may be so. All things are with God.'

71

The Mexicans had camped on the other side of the hills surrounding Pike's Landing. The information they were working on was that the little town was the centre of the gun-running across the Rio Grande, so Lopez and his sergeant had gone to investigate the town. The colonel had a nose for such things and felt at once that those in the cantina were up to no good. All the men were armed and they did not look like farmers or labourers. From certain other indications he concluded that, furthermore, they did not live in this area.

He was convinced that they were just the type of men that he had been instructed to stop. Of course, he knew now that it made no difference to anybody, really, whether or not he tackled the smuggling of arms. However, until he had decided finally what he would do in the future it seemed to do no harm to execute his orders faithfully.

When Colonel Lopez and his sergeant reached the spot where the other men were resting they found, to their surprise, that there was news. A ragged-looking native Mexican was sitting on the ground with the soldiers, talking to them slowly and haltingly. He spoke a strange dialect: a form of Nahuatl which was almost incomprehensible to the men from Mexico. But he was excited and desired greatly to share his news with them. As a result, they too tried their hardest and after a time managed to make out what he was telling them.

It seemed that he lived in a village not far from there, up towards a mission station called San Angelo. Two days previously soldiers had come to the village, searching the villagers' homes and destroying their belongings. The soldiers gave them to understand that some of their number had been ambushed and killed. Many rifles had been stolen and because there were no tracks from the scene of the attack the soldiers had got it into their heads that rebellious Mexicans must have been responsible for it.

'But as the gods live,' said the man, 'we knew nothing. Now my people have gone into the mountains, because we fear that there will be fighting and killing.'

It was impossible to say whether or not the Mexican believed the story that Lopez's men told him: that they were silver miners, peons who had fled their own country and come to the United States in search of work. The colonel gave him a few coins and sent him on his way. Then he gathered his men around him and spoke to them.

'You men know what we are to do. Our intention is to show anybody thinking of transporting arms across the Rio Grande that the game is not worth the reward. It may well be that we shall be forced to make an example of some of these men. It is time that foreigners stopped involving themselves in our affairs.'

There were grunts of approval when Lopez mentioned foreigners. There was not a single one of the men listening to this speech who did not wish to see the Austrian emperor deposed and replaced by a Mexican. Some supported Juarez and others the Conservative church party; all wished to see an end to foreign interference in their country.

After throwing the Mexicans out of the saloon Bob Wheeler was feeling pretty pleased with himself. It was always a pleasure to him to find somebody in a lowlier position than himself and then shove them around a bit. Although he would not have dreamed of challenging Captain Quinnell to his face, over the last few years Wheeler had grown pretty tired of that gentleman's assumption of power and expectations of deference and respect. One of the great advantages that the former sergeant had seen in the scheme of moving to Mexico was that they would all then be on an equal footing; it would not matter a damn who had been an officer and who merely an NCO.

Other patrons were drifting into the bar-room now, mainly farmers who lived hereabouts, together with the odd cowboy. It would be unwise to discuss their business too freely in front of others, so Captain Quinnell signalled to Wheeler with a jerk of his head that he wished to talk outside. When they were in the fresh air, Quinnell said:

'You know what, Bob? It's going to be like the old days when we fetch up in this New Virginia. Why, there's a fellow I used to know before the war, he lived near me. He's growing tobacco and cotton

74

down in Mexico, just like he did in Virginia. Got a bunch of Mexes living in cabins, like the Negroes did on the plantations, you recollect?'

Wheeler grunted non-committally. He'd never owned a plantation, or anything like one. He'd not actually been poor white trash, but it had been damned close to it. He recalled how men like Quinnell had lorded it over his family when he was a child.

'I wouldn't mind having a bunch of Mexes to do the work on some farm I owned,' he said, 'and that's a fact.'

'Good times are coming, Bob, you can bet on it. You know how many of our people are moving south now? You remember "Fighting Joe" Shelby?'

'What, the general?'

'The very same. He's down there now in New Virginia. He's not the only one of our generals who's there, either. Sterling Price, John Magruder, Alexander Terrell, they're all down there now, building up plantations. I tell you, it'll be like the Old South once we get things fairly humming there.'

'When are we goin' to fetch those guns?' asked Wheeler, not being all that keen to talk about various big generals who were now running plantations. 'I'm guessing the cavalry will have gone by now.'

'Happen you're right. You think that tomorrow might be the right time?'

'So I'd think. What about you?'

'Yes, I think that there's no point in delaying further.'

'You have a contact who we're to hand over the weapons to?' Wheeler asked. 'We aren't going to be hawking 'em round El Paso in the marketplace?'

'Lord, but you have a right dry sense of humour,' said Quinnell. 'No, there's a fellow as will meet us down by the river. Meaning the Rio Grande. We can sell him the things and then move on and cross elsewhere. I don't want anybody in the regular Mexican army to catch wind of what we're about. It might not recommend us altogether to the present government, if you take my meaning.'

'So tomorrow it is? We've a cart in that barn. We can use that. I calculate that it'll be a little over a ton and a half's weight, including the ammunition. We're not going to be able to move fast, you know. And not to mention where we're goin' to be powerful vulnerable, when we're a-moving 'cross the country. If some stray army patrol should come across us, I'd say we'll all hang.'

'Like I've said a dozen times before, you're a worrier, Bob. You're right, we're not likely to make any great speed with a cart laden down with over a ton of weaponry, but that's more an inconvenience than a danger. The army don't roam round looking for trouble. They'll think those Henrys are long gone from the area now, I'll be bound.'

'It could be so. Maybe we'll get back tonight, before the men are all drunk as fiddlers' bitches? We'll need to check out that cart and make sure that there's no little repairs need doing.'

'You're right, of course. I should have given some thought to the matter over the last few days. That's why I need you, Bob. You set me right when my mind strays.'

CHAPTER 6

It proved impossible to persuade any of the men to leave the Lucky Lady that night. Bob Wheeler swore at them and Captain Quinnell tried reason, but after being stuck in the farmhouse for two days they were by no means inclined to cut short their drinking session. Not that any of them flatly refused to leave the bar. It was more a question of just one more drink or a final ten minutes. The evening slipped away in this fashion and by the time that they left the men were, just as Wheeler had predicted, hopelessly intoxicated.

They had come on foot to Pike's Landing that evening and although it had only taken an hour and a half to reach the town, it took considerably longer than that to get back to the farmhouse. Bob Wheeler, who was more sober than most of the others and could, in any case, hold his liquor well, was furious with the incapable fools that drink had made of the others.

'Strikes me,' he said angrily, 'that those as can't

hold their drink should sign the pledge and become Methodists or something.'

Those who were in their cups laughed at this as they stumbled and swayed their way back to the farmhouse.

It was partly because of the inebriated condition of most of the men and, consequently, the amount of help that they needed when being assisted to their feet after they had fallen and suchlike, that not one of those making their way from Pike's Landing that night happened to notice that they were being followed.

Perhaps 'followed' is the wrong word. They were being tracked by three men who worked as a team, one behind and two on the flanks, keeping as far from their quarry as they could. They weren't aiming to attack, merely to track these tipsy fools to their lair.

Sergeant Carlos had taken the rear position and directed two of the private soldiers to move along parallel with the party of returning merrymakers. He had sworn a fierce oath that if either of the men was spotted, then he would wreak a terrible revenge upon that person. The men from the fort were a little in awe of Carlos, noting that although he was only a sergeant he was allowed great liberties by the famous Colonel Lopez.

It took three and a half hours for Quinnell's men to get home that night. When they had done so they flopped down in the house and slept where they fell. The three Mexican soldiers gathered together after it was clear that the men had reached their destination.

'Without a doubt,' said Sergeant Carlos, 'this is the rats' nest.'

'What do you make of it?' asked one of the soldiers, 'You believe these men to be smugglers?'

'I believe them to be men who deserve the lightning to fall upon their heads,' replied Carlos vehemently. 'I do not think that we need look further if we wish to set an example and show these Anglos that it is time to stop poking their snouts into our affairs.'

One of the other men was also a native Mexican and he muttered to Carlos in *Nahuatl*:

'We need the guns the foreigners sell to us.'

'That is where you are wrong,' replied the sergeant in the same language. 'But do not concern yourself with such high matters. Trust me, we do not need these men. You may kill them with an easy heart.'

The only men in the farmhouse who were anything like approaching sober were Quinnell and Wheeler. After the others had more or less collapsed and were breathing heavily and, in some cases, snoring, Quinnell offered Bob Wheeler a cigar. The two of them sat talking quietly by the glow of a single oil lamp.

When Carlos and the other men arrived back at the little camp, which they did not until it was nearly dawn, it was to find everybody but Colonel Lopez asleep. The men from the fort were told to rest at once and Carlos gave the colonel a brief account of what they had found. They spoke quietly and confidentially.

'You understand,' Lopez said, 'why I am fixed in my purpose of dealing with these people and discouraging others from smuggling? Even though it makes no difference to the situation, now that the Americans are going to supply Juarez with all the weaponry he requires?'

'But of course, my Colonel,' replied Carlos. 'Even if you wish to take up the President's offer of commanding his forces, you would not have it thought that you played Maximilian false. You undertook this mission for the Emperor and you will fulfil it, pointless though it now turns out to be. Otherwise, you will feel that you betrayed your trust.'

'Well then, knowing this, be content. I may yet return to Mexico City and deal with this evil that faces our people. Perhaps I can do more good being at the heart of Maximilian's power. Who knows?'

At first light Colonel Lopez had Carlos rouse the men and when they had broken their fast he spoke to them.

'If what that man who told us of this business when the Yankee cavalry were attacked spoke truth,' he said, 'then a large quantity of arms are to carried over the Rio Grande in the next few days. I guess that those who were drinking in the cantina last night do not have a steamboat and I also suppose that they will not be riding up to El Paso with their haul, if indeed it was they who stole the guns.

'Here is what I would know. How could one pass many rifles across the river near here?'

There was dead silence from the soldiers and Lopez noticed one or two of them exchanging glances. He went on impatiently:

'I too was once an ordinary soldier. I would take oath that you men know where and how things are brought across the border. Not guns perhaps, but of a certainty tobacco and liquor. Where and how is it done in these parts?'

At last, after some whispering between the men, one of them spoke.

'Colonel,' he said, 'it is useless to try and hide anything from your keen sight. You are like an eagle—'

Lopez cut in, a faint smile playing around his mouth, saying:

'Spare me the compliments, my man. Just tell me what method is like to be used if a heavy weight is to be carried from one shore of the river to the other.'

'Well then,' the soldier replied, 'there are two brothers who live by the Rio Grande, one on either side. They have a rope, which lies on the riverbed and is fixed, one end on the bank on the Yankee side and one on ours.

'When they wish, they raise this rope high above the Rio Grande and then use pulleys to move goods across the river. But I swear on my honour, we none of us ever heard of them carrying arms across.'

'What are the usual goods?' asked Colonel Lopez, smiling. 'Tobacco? Whiskey?'

'Even so, sir.'

'You have seen this pulley in operation?'

The man nodded slightly.

'Would it hold, say, five rifles at a time?'

'Without a doubt, sir.'

Lopez looked at the men seated before him and felt that he might risk being a little more open with them. He actually wished for them to cooperate with what he was proposing to do and he knew very well the kind of mulish obstinacy that would enable even common soldiers like these to slow down his work, or even entirely frustrate his purposes.

'I am sure you men would be happy to see any number of guns enter our country,' he said, 'if they were to be used to drive out Maximilian and the French. I give you my word that this enterprise will not stop weapons reaching our esteemed former president. There now, have I your cooperation?'

There were nods and even a few smiles. It was seldom enough that these soldiers met a high-ranking officer who seemed to understand them as this colonel did. Moreover, was he not a native Mexican?

Seeing that he had brought them over to his side, Lopez spoke again:

'I wish for two men to go and watch those Anglos, those who were drinking last night. Most like, they have the stolen weapons up at their house, hidden away in a hole, perhaps.' He turned to Carlos and said, 'How long would it take a man moving swiftly, to reach that farmhouse?'

'If he moved at good speed, then no more than an

hour and a half.'

'From all that I am able to apprehend, they were last night hopelessly drunk. They will not be rising soon. If two men set out now they would be able to reach their house before anything has been done about the guns.'

Within fifteen minutes two men had been dispatched north. They were to stake out the house where the Confederates were staying. Once confirmation was received that they were indeed engaged in trading in arms, then one man was to return at once to give warning and the other was to remain there, spying on them.

So far, since crossing the Rio Grande into Texas, Lopez and his group of men had had no misfortunes and the expedition still seemed like a harmless little adventure. All of the men knew, of course, that at some point they would probably be called upon to kill – and perhaps be killed themselves in turn – but there was no sign yet of any such unpleasantness.

One of the men sent off to spy on the farmhouse was feeling particularly pleased with himself. Enrique Calderon was just nineteen years of age and had only recently joined the army. He was a Mexican peasant and becoming a soldier was the only way that he was ever likely to see any more of the wide world than the scrubby and barren fields that surrounded the village in which he had grown up.

Now, here he was, a soldier of the Emperor on a secret mission in the United States. The stories he would have to tell when he went home on furlough!

He little knew that he was destined to become the first casualty of the affair and that he had barely two hours of life left to him.

Enrique Calderon and his companion reached the farmhouse in a little under an hour and a half but were only just in time to see the men staying at the house hauling out a cart. The two young men peered cautiously over the low stone wall, which stretched for a hundred feet from the barn. The men were too busy and suffering too badly from the ill effects of their overindulgence the night before to notice them. While a couple of them were harnessing a horse to the rickety-looking old wagon, the others were tacking up horses. Within twenty minutes of Enrique and his companion arriving the place was deserted.

Enrique Calderon stood up. His comrade, Luis Gortari, hissed a warning:

'What if they are not all gone? What then?'

'Ah, you woman! Are you then afraid?'

Gortari got to his feet. Since nobody shouted or, worse still, shot at them from the house, he began to think that his friend was right not to fear anything. Enrique continued, growing more confident:

'Listen, one of us should follow those men on foot. We cannot catch them up, but the dust from that cart will mark their track for miles ahead. Then the other can search the house and carry back a report to the colonel.'

'And you would have me enter the house and be caught there, I think.'

'By no means,' said Enrique contemptuously. 'I will ransack their lair if you follow them and see what you can find. That place, San Angelo, is not far from here. Perhaps they make for that.'

Faced with a choice between a brisk trot across the country and being caught like a rat in a trap in somebody's house, perhaps by others who were not in that main party or who might come back to the house unexpectedly, Luis Gortari chose to follow the Anglos and see what they were about. It was a decision that was to save his life.

The two men parted amiably enough. Enrique went, notwithstanding his bravado, with some trepidation to search the farmhouse. He could have saved himself the trouble, for there was nothing in there that gave any indication of what the men had been about. Certainly there were guns aplenty, including some strange rifles with brass tubes affixed to the tops of their barrels, but no 400-repeating rifles.

He gave up in disgust after half an hour and left the building, undecided as to whether he should follow Luis and try to catch him up, wait here for his return, or go back to the others. He had not the faintest notion that he had only thirty minutes to live.

It was the merest chance circumstance that sealed the fate of young Enrique Calderon. Had the cavalry patrol arrived half an hour earlier they would most likely have ignored him and focused all their attentions upon the bunch of former Confederate

86

soldiers occupying the farmhouse. Seeing so many Southerners hitching up a wagon and preparing to ride north towards San Angelo would certainly have captured their interest more than a Mexican youth.

Quinnell and his men had been deceiving themselves when they concluded that only two days or so would be quite sufficient for the US Cavalry at Las Cruces to give up on wondering who had massacred seven of their comrades so brutally. There had been a number of ambushes of Union forces in both Texas and Louisiana over the last six months and the authorities were very much inclined to blame some wandering band of 'Diehards'.

Only the fact that after the attack at San Angelo the killers had apparently vanished into thin air persuaded those investigating the business that perhaps native Mexicans were at the back of it. Otherwise they would, as a matter of course, have assumed that it was the work of Confederates who were unwilling to concede that the war had ended.

A particular and unfortunate point about the attack at San Angelo was that one of the officers at Las Cruces had lost his younger brother, who had been in charge of the detail bringing the rifles up into New Mexico. The boy was twenty-one years of age and had only recently been commissioned. Heading the escort on the weapons being taken up to the arsenal had been his very first independent action in command of men in the field, and his big brother had been looking forward to greeting him when he arrived at Las Cruces.

As a result of the death of this lad Captain Michael Sullivan had been riding the range around San Angelo in ever increasing circles for the last three days, hoping to catch the scent of those responsible for his kid brother's death.

Needless to say, Enrique Calderon knew nothing of all this when he left the house he had lately been searching, only to find that six riders had arrived at precisely the moment when he stepped blinking into the sunlight. They were, by the look of them, Yankee soldiers.

It was a delicate situation, because of course Enrique was not in uniform and by any definition was little better than a spy. Captain Sullivan and his men had come upon the house by sheer chance. Having seen it, they thought that it would be worth asking the inhabitants if they had seen or heard anything of note.

'What we got here?' asked Captain Sullivan. 'Mex, by the look of you. What are you about in that house? You live there?'

Now another circumstance that did nothing to help young Enrique was that he had only the most superficial acquaintance with the English language. His native tongue was Nahuatl and he could speak Spanish fluently, but English he could barely understand, let alone discourse in.

'No my house,' managed Calderon. 'No live here.'

'You don't live there, hey?' said Sullivan, his eyes narrowing. 'I guess you were thieving, then. What have you in that pack of yours? Goods that you were about to carry off?'

'No,' said the wretched young man. 'I mine, I dig. This my tools.'

'Tools, hey?' said the the captain. 'Let's see 'em then. Empty your bag.'

'Ah, come on, sir,' said his sergeant. 'We ain't the police, nor nothing' like. What do we care if he's been a looting of that house?'

Captain Sullivan made no reply because already the young man was emptying out his pack. At once it could be seen that the bag contained not silver coffee pots or snuff boxes or anything else that might have been stolen for its monetary value, but rather a small arsenal of weaponry. A dismantled carbine tumbled out, followed by a Colt Navy pistol, a bag of balls, some loose cartridges and a flask of powder. There was enough to compromise a chameleon.

At the sight of the guns Sullivan forgot all about the possibility of former soldiers of the Confederacy conducting a private war. He recollected that he had also wondered whether native Mexicans had been responsible for the murders of his brother and the other men, so mysteriously had the attackers succeeded in spiriting away over a ton of weaponry without the use of a horse and cart. He spoke to one of his men:

'Reach me up the parts of that carbine there. I'll warrant it's a Sharps.'

The rifle did indeed turn out to be a Sharps 52-calibre carbine, of the very same kind that the troopers had been carrying at San Angelo. The bodies had been looted and their side arms removed. Without a shadow of a doubt, thought Captain Sullivan, this was one of those very carbines, stolen from the dead after the ambush.

'Where d'you get this?' he asked the frightened youth, who made no answer. 'I'll tell you where you got it, shall I? You took it from a body. Body of one o' my men.'

The young Mexican soldier just about understood what he was accused of, but did not have enough English words to rebut the accusation. Instead, he responded in a flood of Nahuatl and that sealed his fate. Captian Sullivan spoke to his sergeant:

'There's a hoist nigh to the roof of that barn. Take two men and fix a rope over it.'

'You ain't goin' to take him for questioning, sir?'

'Not a bit if it. He's not going to answer any questions. I gave him a chance. Mark what I say, this is one of those who killed our men up at the defile. One at least of them will pay.'

Sergeant Brewster dismounted and ordered two of the troopers to assist him. Between them they threaded a stout rope through the pulley on the old hoist and then, when it was dangling at the correct height, they fashioned a noose on it, which they left hanging some eight or nine feet from the ground., They tied the other end of the rope to the roof beam of the barn.

Sullivan addressed the terrified man, who had watched these preparations in mounting disbelief:

'I'm giving you one last chance. You tell me how you came by a cavalry carbine and I might take you to Las Cruces for questioning, rather than hanging you on the spot.'

'I have Sharps, because I too soldier. I am in army.'

Captain Sullivan had heard enough and did not propose to waste any more time on this lying savage.

'Set him on a horse and put that rope round his neck,' he ordered.

It took the combined strength of Sergeant Brewster and two strong men to drag Calderon, struggling, kicking and screaming, over to where the noose awaited him. There was then another fight before they could lash his hands behind his back with a rawhide thong and get him on a horse. Sullivan dismounted and himself slapped the horse's rump to send him skittering off, leaving the Mexican to kick out his life on the end of the rope.

It seemed to Captain Sullivan that perhaps he had evened up the score just a little for the death of his younger brother.

CHAPTER 7

'How long shall we wait here?' Sergeant Carlos asked the colonel. 'We all need a proper meal in our bellies. There's a limit to how long one can live on these emergency rations.'

'I've given that thought. We are going to visit that little town again, the one where I was treated so discourteously.'

'You still hold a grudge for that, my Colonel? But the man who delivered that kick is no longer there. He will be with those who are, we hope, even now being tracked by those two young men.'

Lopez laughed quietly. 'My pride is not the motive for saying that we will go again to the town of Pike's Landing. It is famous for being a stopping place for gunrunners. Our job is to make an example of such men and show that they, and those who help them, may expect no end of trouble.'

'What then?'

'Those two who went off, Calderon and Gortari was it? They cannot be back here in less than four hours. In three we can reach Pike's Landing, do what is needful and then come back here and be ready to meet up again with our scouts.'

'What is needful?' asked Carlos. 'I do not understand. What are we to do at that place?'

Colonel Lopez explained what he had in mind and even the sergeant, who had accompanied his master on any number of occasions and knew more than most just how ruthless Lopez really was, was a little shocked. There were those in Mexico City who regarded Colonel Lopez as some sort of effete dandy. If only those people could be here now and hear what this elegant ladies' man was intending to do to the sleepy little town where he had been so shamefully treated, it would go a long way towards changing their view of the man.

Before they set out for Pike's Landing Colonel Lopez desired Carlos to order the men to assemble their carbines, load and prime them and then prepare for action.

Quinnell's men could only proceed north at a snail's pace, burdened as they were with the horse and cart. In fact, the fleet-footed Gortari might well have been able to overtake the party had he been minded to do so. His chief fear was of being seen by the men whose footsteps he was dogging, but here he was fortunate enough to be favoured by the topography of the area. A ridge of land ran alongside the road to San Angelo, parallel to the track and some 200 feet from it. By moving swiftly along on the other side of this high ground, alternately running for a hundred paces then walking briskly for the same number, Gortari found that he was able to keep abreast of the group of Anglos. From time to time he would stop and then crawl up the slope on his hands and knees, to peep over the top and make sure that his quarry was still in view and pursuing the same course.

By the time they reached their destination even Gortari, who was an agile and fit young man at the very peak of his physical strength, had had enough and was ready to rest. The road snaked into a range of rugged hills and Luis Gortari was wondering how he might be able to follow the men unobtrusively through the narrow defile ahead. Fortunately they halted before entering the pass and the men dismounted and began smoking.

It seemed to the young soldier that this was the place for which they had been heading, but what there could be here that was so important to them he was quite unable to say. He continued to watch, his head just poking over the top of the ridge.

After a space, when the men were rested a little, they began to manoeuvre the wagon and turn it round. Then, they coaxed the horse into backing up. It was evidently their intention to take the cart backwards into the little pass ahead of them. It took no great effort of the brain to see that the intention was to load it up with something and then bring that same load out of the defile. Presumably, thought Gortari, the track was too narrow to make turning round an easy manoeuvre when once they entered the space between the towering crags.

The horses were left tethered to a clump of bristlecone pines. Incredible to relate, not one of the men stayed behind to guard their mounts. Every single one of them followed the wagon as it slowly reversed into the miniature canyon.

Luis Gortari now showed the first flash of the brilliance that would, once the French army had left his country, propel him from being a humble private soldier towards becoming in later years a high-ranking officer.

In the distance he could see a little white-painted building; without doubt it was a mission station. Then, in an instant, the whole matter became plain to him. This area must be the San Angelo that the Mexican had talked of, the place where the cavalry claimed that many of their rifles had been stolen. Without knowing the particulars of the thing, Gortari saw now that for a certainty the men he had been trailing had come here to retrieve those weapons, load them on to that cart and then take them to the crossing point on the Rio Grande.

Before acting, the young Mexican carefully went over the steps in his reasoning, looking for a weak link. He could find none; he knew then that he had to move at once.

He stood up and walked quickly down the slope to where the horses were tethered. He unhitched one at random and led it to the road. Then he swung himself into the saddle and set off at a trot. After a minute or two, throwing caution to the winds, he urged the creature into a canter; then, almost at once, to a gallop. He would have to hope that by the time that those villains had completed their business in the pass he would be far enough away for it to be quite impossible for them to catch him.

The inhabitants of Pike's Landing lived almost wholly on the illicit proceeds of smuggling and criminal activity of one sort and another. The town had been established in this location, right on the border between two territories, for that very purpose, the forces of law and order in Texas thinking it easy to pretend that it was in New Mexico, or, when convenient, vice versa.

Nobody showed any enthusiasm for cleaning the place up, so consequently it was the haunt of gunrunners, whiskey-smugglers, those dealing illegally in gold, and various other types who passed through, having been on the scout in one part of the territories or the other.

Most such settlements had at least an informal system for maintaining law and order, even if it was just a vigilance committee. Pike's Landing had no such lawkeeper. It was lawless to an alarming degree; if the inhabitants made a good profit from the men who used their town as a refuge they also had to put up with a certain level of violence and disorder on their streets, even in their store and their saloon.

By and large, however, the victims of the beatings, knifings and even occasional shootings were other bad men, rather than those who lived in the town. It might aptly be said that Pike's Landing thrived on the proceeds of crime and that its citizens, in consequence, turned a blind eye to where the money that flowed so freely through their hands had come from.

Colonel Lopez knew all about towns like Pike's Landing. There were a few similar little spots on the border between Mexico and the United States: El Paso, for example. He had little sympathy for those who consented to wrongdoing because it brought them a financial reward; therefore he had no qualms about the enterprise upon which he was about to embark. As his little squad bore down on Pike's Landing, Lopez spoke to his sergeant:

'You apprehend why I am scrupulously carrying out the last instruction that I received from his Imperial Majesty?'

'I believe so,' said Carlos. 'You hope to save your honour if, when we are done, you join forces with His Excellency the President.'

'You mean the former president. Recollect that we no longer have a president, but instead are blessed with an emperor. But you speak truly about my honour. The Emperor entrusted me with a mission, which was to make an example of those running guns to the rebels across the border and to make sure that men on this side of the Rio Grande were discouraged from such practices.

'I told Maximilian that I would do so, and I would be a faithless dog indeed if after leaving his presence

I joined up at once with his mortal enemy. No, I will do what I promised to do and then we shall see in what direction the wind blows.'

Only a man who had spent years in the service of the colonel would have had the temerity to ask the question that Carlos now came out with:

'But truly, my Colonel, did that kick up your hindquarters not influence this action that we are taking now? Not in any degree?'

Far from being annoyed Colonel Lopez was secretly amused at the effrontery of the man; he even deigned to smile slightly.

'It is seldom enough, Carlos,' he said, 'that a man is able to combine duty and pleasure with such enthusiasm. So you yourself remarked but a short time ago. It is indeed my duty to make an example of this pest-hole, but I do not deny that I shall gain great pleasure from doing so.'

Only fifty or sixty people actually lived permanently in Pike's Landing; the rest of those found in the town were transients of one type and another. Sometimes such men would show up, rent a house and live there for a week, a month or even longer. More commonly, men would stay for only one or two nights. On this day there were only half a dozen strangers staying in the town.

The Mexicans marched straight to the Lucky Lady, where they found eight men drinking. Under the levelled carbines of the eight soldiers, all the men present, albeit with considerable reluctance and many protests, relinquished their guns, piling them up on the floor. Then Colonel Lopez, the only member of the party who spoke reasonable English, asked the barkeep if he had a large can of lamp oil.

The man stared at Lopez in utter amazement.

'You're holdin' us up for lamp oil?' he asked in disbelief.

'Just fetch it,' said Lopez. 'One of my men will go with you, to forestall treachery.'

The drinkers who had had their pistols confiscated watched to see what would happen next. Although the men with the rifles were dressed as Mexican peasants, it was obvious that there was a little more to the case than a simple robbery. They were soon rewarded for their curiosity when the barkeep arrived back under escort, struggling with a two-gallon drum of kerosene.

At a word from Carlos two men relieved the owner of the saloon of his burden, then began splashing the liquid liberally around, over the furniture and floor of the place. They also sprinkled some over the heap of weaponry that had been taken from the patrons.

'Hey, what's the idea?' called out one of the prisoners. 'Surely you ain't goin' to burn us alive?'

'Rest assured,' said Colonel Lopez, 'it is nothing of the sort. We are only showing this town what misfortune will fall like lightning upon the heads of those who aid men running guns into Mexico. We look to men such as yourselves to spread the word, far and wide.'

Having completed his little speech Lopez took a

box of lucifers from his pocket, lit one and tossed it on to a chair which had been soaked in lamp oil. In a few seconds sooty orange flames engulfed the piece of furniture, sending a plume of greasy black smoke up to the ceiling.

'Those of you who would live had best come out at once,' said Lopez.

The men were shepherded from the barroom at gunpoint. Once the building was blazing merrily the colonel led his men across the street to the general store. Their appearance in the premises created a sensation.

'Holy Moses!' muttered the old man behind the counter. 'It's an invasion.' The customers said nothing, nor did they move. The sight of eight soldiers, lined up like a firing squad and all aiming their carbines at the five or six men and women waiting to be served by the clerk, acted to discourage precipitate action.

'We require some meat, coffee, bread and cheese,' explained Colonel Lopez courteously. 'If you simply place these items on the counter there, my associate will collect them.'

The clerk gaped in utter astonishment at this request, as well he might. At last he said:

'You come here to rob us of ham and cheese? You don't want my money too?'

'By no means,' replied Lopez. 'We are not thieves. Only stark necessity would compel me to deprive you of these comestibles.'

'Don't he talk fine for a foreigner?' observed a

100

middle-aged woman. 'Why, it's as good as a play to hear him speak!'

As the man placed upon the counter the items which the colonel had named, so Carlos collected them and put them in his pack. He then moved around, depositing the remander in the backpacks of the other soldiers, who still kept their weapons trained upon the customers of the store.

Outside in the street there was a slowly growing hubbub of shouting and running footsteps. Lopez spoke to the old man who had just served them the food:

'And now, you have a can of lamp oil, perhaps?'

'Gallon, half-gallon, pint?'

'A gallon, if you please.'

When the kerosene had been produced Sergeant Carlos took charge of it and at once began sprinkling it on anything that looked as though it might readily take fire: bales of cloth, wooden tools and suchlike. The owner of the store watched this proceeding with growing alarm.

'What's the idea?' he asked.

'The idea,' replied the colonel politely, 'is this. There is to be no more smuggling of arms across the border into Mexico. Be sure to tell your friends and neighbours of this. Now, unless you wish to be roasted alive, I would suggest that you all leave.'

'Hey, you can't do that,' cried the old man. 'This here's my livelihood. What'll I do if you torch my store?'

'You might have thought of that before you

started encouraging bandits and other types to linger in your town and buy your wares,' explained Colonel Lopez. He lit a match. As his men marched the civilians out at gunpoint, Lopez dropped the match on to a bale of cloth, which at once took fire.

So far everything had been going the soldiers' way and there had been no sort of opposition. It was not to be expected that this state of affairs would last indefinitely; as they retreated from the burning store a shot was fired in their direction from an upstairs window. At once three of the men returned fire, shattering the window glass and giving them the satisfaction of hearing a yell of pain.

Now that the shooting had begun the men's military training took over and they began acting like soldiers in hostile territory. The civilians in the street fled for cover, not wishing to be caught in the crossfire.

There came more scattered shots. Carlos took command of the squad of men, scanning the windows to see where the fire was coming from, then directing the men as to their targets. Colonel Lopez stood near by, a sad look upon his face. It had been a dreadful thing, as the storekeeper had suggested, to deprive men of their means of making a living, but then again, these people must have known well enough the sort of people that their little town's prosperity was dependent upon.

There was the sporadic crackle of small-arms fire as the Mexicans traded shots with various people living in or visiting Pike's Landing. It was an unequal contest because those firing at the Mexicans were armed with pistols and were, moreover, some distance from their targets. For their own part, the Mexicans were trained soldiers, armed with military carbines, which could be sighted up to several hundred yards. The shooting gradually died down as it became clear that the invaders had the better armaments.

In the meantime the saloon and general store were blazing fiercely despite the efforts of those throwing pails of water on the flames. Now that the firing had stopped people drifted into the street to see what was going on. Lopez took the opportunity to make an announcement.

'You citizens had best take heed of what you have seen this day,' he said in a loud voice. 'Anybody who deals in weapons or tries to interfere in the affairs of the Mexican people will pay a heavy price. This day's work has been as nothing compared with what will come next.'

Having said this the colonel ordered Carlos to organize the men and prepare to leave the town licking its wounds. Nobody else seemed disposed to fire at them or organize any opposition, so Sergeant Carlos formed the men into double ranks and they marched out of Pike's Landing in good order.

As may readily be imagined, the men of the town rode off to summon aid almost as soon as the soldiers had left. They found, though, that neither the sheriff of the nearby Texas town of Endurance nor the military authorities at Las Cruces showed the slightest interest in hearing of their misfortunes.

The citizens of Pike's Landing had danced between the raindrops for so long, harbouring all manner of undesirable types, that nobody was minded to come to their assistance. The most the sheriff would say was that he would ride over and look into the matter when he had time, although, he added, he recollected that on a previous occasion he had been assured by the townsfolk that Pike's Landing lay under the protection of the New Mexico Territory.

The army in Las Cruces was even less sympathetic, having already lost seven of its men to a gang whom they strongly suspected of having been sheltering in or near to Pike's Landing.

'You fellows want help from us,' said Major Watkins, 'Then you can make a start by turfing out all the comancheros, gunrunners, bandits and other low men from that town of yours. Then you can appoint a vigilance committee or, better still, vote in a sheriff. When you've done all that come by my base again and we'll have a nice talk.'

That was all the comfort that the men from Pike's Landing received. They had lost four men in the raid and had also seen their saloon and store burned to the ground. It was a salutary lesson though, because after the town recovered from the unfortunate incidents of that day, things did begin to change somewhat.

*

The squad of Mexicans were perhaps three miles from Pike's Landing when they were met by Luis Gortari, who came riding up on the fine chestnut mare that he had stolen up at San Angelo.

He had two pieces of news. The first was that a bunch of men who had been staying in a farmhouse not far from the town had taken a wagon up to the pass through the hills, probably with a view to bringing some heavy load back in this direction.

The second was that as he was riding back from the pass as fast as he was able he had passed that same farmhouse and seen one of their comrades hanging from the barn.

'I think,' said Colonel Lopez, 'that we will now proceed to the Rio Grande. We are going to move very fast and it seems to me that we might outrun a heavily laden wagon. I doubt those men are going to be racing.

'We will march for another hour and then make a hearty meal of the provisions that the good people of Pike's Landing were kind enough to donate for our needs.'

The men were halted, as the colonel had promised, after another hour's march. From all that Lopez was able to apprehend they were well ahead of the men who would most likely be coming this way with the stolen rifles. Those men would be unlikely to be in any hurry to reach the river. From what he had now heard from young Luis Gortari, they would in all probability stop at their farmhouse to collect their belongings. With good fortune,

Lopez and his men should be the first to reach the point where the smugglers meant to transfer the goods across into Mexico. They would then have the time and leisure to arrange a little surprise for the Anglos when they arrived.

CHAPTER 8

Loading up the cart with the Henrys was not as easy and straightforward as Quinnell and his boys might have hoped. The wagon in which the cavalry had been transporting their weaponry had been custom-built for the job. Piling a ton-and-a-half weight on to this rickety old buckboard required careful planning; the weight had to be precisely, evenly distributed or the cart began leaning to one side in the most precarious manner. It would be a disaster if it were to overturn, perhaps becoming damaged, on the road to the Rio Grande.

One of the men expressed the view of several when he said irritably:

'Hell's afire, can't we just say be damned to this and make tracks for New Virginia, right this minute?'

'You have shit for brains or what, Patterson?' Bob Wheeler responded sharply. 'How much cash money do you have in your pocket right now?'

'I couldn't rightly say. Twenty, maybe thirty

dollars. Why?'

' 'Cause we got to make our way down through Mexico to New Virginia. Then we got to sign up with the army and serve for a spell before we get any pay. I'd be surprised if we see any cash for upwards of a month or two. How d'you expect to live during that time?'

'I guess we could do us a little bushwhackin''—'

'God almighty!' cried Wheeler in despair. 'That'd make a fine beginning in the country we're aimin' to call home! Just load up that wagon and keep your mouth closed.'

Eventually the weapons were loaded, balanced delicately on the cart. There was only one pair of light shafts, such as would accommodate a single horse. The task of drawing the vehicle proved only just possible for this animal, so heavily laden was it with armament.

When they got back to the entrance to the pass they discovered that one of their horses had been stolen. There were bitter recriminations from Jim Patterson, whose mount it was that had been taken, and questions as to why nobody had thought to set a guard to stand sentry-go over the beasts.

'There's no manner of use fretting over who should have done what and when,' declared Captain Quinnell. 'We must make the best of it. There's a spare horse back at the house, recollect. You can drive the wagon, Patterson.'

It was a mighty slow journey back to the farm-house, because the horse was labouring under such a heavy load. The rest of the crew felt that it would be a scurvy trick to play were they to ride on ahead and leave their comrade to plod along at a snail's pace. There was also a more practical reason for them to stick with the wagon, which was that they were very much depending upon the money that those rifles would bring from the followers of Juarez.

They had no way of knowing that the whole enterprise was now a fool's errand. The men who had previously agreed a price for the weapons with Quinnell would not be likely to pay a single cent for them now; not since the news had reached them that the government in Washington was minded to arm the rebels for free. There were already consignments of guns and ammunition on the way south to El Paso, where the local army commander was under orders to find a convenient way of 'losing' them to the Mexican rebels.

Even after all the trouble and deaths that the Henry rifles had cost, it was not worth anybody's while to transport them down to the border now.

None of this was known, of course, to the captain and his men as they crawled along the road south from San Angelo. So when they reached the house that had been their home for a while they received a terrible shock.

There, hanging above the door of the barn, was a man who had obviously died an excruciatingly painful death. His face was contorted in agony and suffused with blood. In his final agony he had bitten through his own tongue and the blood from this wound had run down his chin and stained his bleached cotton smock.

'What do you make of that, Bob?' asked Captain Quinnell in a low voice.

'I'd say it's an Indian, maybe Mexican. Beyond that, I wouldn't care to go.'

'I meant to say, who would hang a man here? You think it's a warning to us?'

'It could be so,' said Wheeler thoughtfully. 'You want we should get him down and see if there's any clues to be found?'

Barnabas Quinnell was looking up at the hanged man as though he was a portent of doom. He could not for the life of him have said how, but he was convinced that this death was connected in some way with the guns they had seized from the army. Like so many who rode on the wrong side of the law, Quinnell had a superstitious streak: he felt in his waters that this was a bad omen.

There proved to be nothing on the body to identify who the man was or at whose hands he had met his death. On the face of it the business looked like a lynching, but there was something about it that made all the men uneasy. Why choose to hang the fellow near their own house? The finding of the dead body cast something of a dampener on the spirits of all the men: they moved about quietly and thoughtfully for the rest of the day, fearful that a death of this sort, so close to their habitation, might be a sign that their own deaths were imminent.

*

110

Colonel Lopez and his squad of men were making faster progress than the men trying to move the guns to the border. After their meal they marched and ran until the moon had risen. They rested for ten minutes in every hour, but for the rest of the time the pace was ferocious.

The colonel was not one to demand more of others than he himself gave and he was always the last to sit down and first to rise during their periods of rest.

When it was quite dark Lopez ordered a halt and said that they might build a fire to warm themselves and then eat the remains of the food that they had acquired in Pike's Landing.

'At this speed,' Carlos said to the colonel, 'we shall reach the Rio Grande a little after noon tomorrow.'

'That is my hope.'

'What then, sir?'

'We deal with the smugglers there and then wait for the men who stole those rifles.'

'Have we not done all that you offered to the Emperor? Could we not just cross the river ourselves with no further action?'

'Why, Carlos,' said the colonel, 'I have never yet known you to be afraid. Don't tell me that you fear those bandits?'

'I fear nobody, my Colonel. Not even the Devil himself.' At this point Sergeant Carlos crossed himself, recalling the lessons drummed into him at the mission school.

'It is not fear,' he went on, 'but a fierce desire to

remain alive long enough to see the rightful leader of our country take his place in the presidential palace. Just think, a true Mexican leading us once more!'

'How then if I return to Mexico City and take up Maximilian's offer of leading his army? Will we find ourselves fighting on opposite sides? Imagine, I shall defend the Emperor against you, who will lead the rebels in their final assault. That would be a strange circumstance indeed.'

Carlos, who knew when Colonel Lopez was being serious and when not, laughed at that.

'*Ai*,' he said, 'that would be a sad day indeed, sir.'

They all slept peacefully that night and Lopez did not even think it necessary to set sentries to guard them as they slumbered.

The next day, Carlos roused the men at first light and, after breaking their fast on a few leftovers from the previous evening's meal, they began marching to the Rio Grande.

Shortly after the beginning of the War Between the States two men had settled in Texas, right on the banks of the Rio Grande. Leastways, one had settled on the north bank, which was on the Texas side of the river, while the other, after certain arrangements had been made, made his abode on the other side of the river, in Mexico.

Jake and Pete Frobisher were brothers and they had a surefire plan to turn a little profit from the war that was about to engulf their nation. It was nothing

112

grand; they were not greedy men. All that they required was enough to buy a little liquor and tobacco, with maybe a few dollars left over to play the odd game of poker.

They built themselves little houses, really no better than huts, one on each side of the river. They then managed to get a stout rope fixed up, with one end firmly fixed to a tree in Texas and the other similarly placed in Mexico. All that was then needful was to let this rope lie on the riverbed when not in use.

At first Jake and Pete just used little pulley-wheels on the rope when it was stretched tight, secured little bags of tobacco and bottles of whiskey on to them, and pulled the goods across from the American side to Mexico. The duty in Mexico was prohibitively high and they found regular buyers for their wares.

From these small beginnings the brothers moved on to other things, such as guns, gold and anything else that a body might wish to transfer from one country to another without having to answer any awkward questions about the transaction.

By the summer of 1865 the Frobishers were doing so well out of their little business that they were thinking of giving it up and moving elsewhere. The problem was that they had become simply too well-known. After transferring a fair quantity of weaponry across the Rio Grande for Juarez's men, Jake, who lived on the Mexican side of the river, was beginning to get nervy and worry that Maximilian's forces might arrive in the north in large numbers, put him up against a wall and shoot him.

It was not a fanciful fear. He did quite a bit of business with the soldiers from the nearby fort at Cueda, but they only wanted liquor. They certainly had no idea that he was running guns across the border.

Pete Frobisher, for his part, was also getting somewhat jumpy. Now that the war was over between North and South, you might have expected that there would be less military activity in the area, but that wasn't at all the case. In fact patrols along the road that ran parallel to the river were now a regular sight; one or two had even stopped by Pete's place, asking if he had seen this or that individual.

Luckily no one stopped by when he and his brother had their rope up and were ferrying stuff from one bank to the other, but it was only a matter of time until they were caught red-handed at their activities.

The Mexicans who had dealt such a harsh lesson to the town of Pike's Landing arrived at the Rio Grande looking, once again, like wandering peasants. They had dismantled their carbines after the gun battle and stowed them back in their packs. It would have been a shrewd man indeed who could have spotted that here was a detachment of the Mexican army on active service.

'Hey, you men!' shouted Pete Frobisher, a mite irritably when he spotted them approaching his little stone-built home. 'What are you about here? This here's private property, I'd have you know.'

This was of course a complete and barefaced lie, but what would a bunch of vagabond native Mexicans know of such matters? The men halted uncertainly and looked around, apparently unsure of what to do next. A man in early middle age approached Pete where he lazed fishing by the river.

'A thousand pardons, señor,' he said apologetically. 'We did not mean to trespass. It is that we are become lost. Is this the road to El Paso?'

Pete laughed at that.

'Well, you keep on down the way for some five hundred miles, it is. Take you a fair time to cover on foot, though.'

The man's face fell in dismay and he stepped a little closer. Pete Frobisher was wearing a pair of .45s; he looked like the kind of man who knew how to handle them and would have no compunction about doing so. The Mexican in front of him was so comical, obviously posing no threat to him, that Frobisher didn't even trouble to take his hands from the fishing rod as he talked.

Not until the man he was talking to was standing right before him did the danger become clear; the Mexican reached behind him and pulled out a single-action pistol that he had evidently had tucked in the back of his pants. Cocking it with his thumb as he drew down on Pete Frobisher, the man said in quite a different tone from the one he had lately been using:

'Make one move towards your weapons and you are a dead man.'

He called to one of the others, who sauntered forward and removed Frobisher's guns from their holsters.

'Now we will have a little conversation, you and I,' said the Mexican in English that bore scarcely a trace of an accent, 'and then we shall see if you live or die.'

This all sounded mighty unpromising to the smuggler, who now began to think that his last day had come. Although not a religious man he thought that a prayer or two might be in order. Before he had a chance to test this notion Colonel Lopez continued:

'We have a little business to conduct with some men who, we believe, are coming here to avail themselves of your services. We shall bind you hand and foot and leave you in that hut of yours. If you call a warning or attempt to escape we shall kill you without compunction. Otherwise, if you lie still and quiet, we will free you when we have finished what we purpose to do here this day. What do you say?'

'What do I say?' asked Pete, immensely relieved. 'Why, I say just you tie me up now and I'll engage to lie as quiet as a babe in arms until you've finished whatever it is that you're up to.'

Over on the other bank of the mighty river Jake Frobisher observed all of this exchange with great misgiving. It seemed to him that the dozen or so men who had descended upon his brother's home were not planning to murder him out of hand. Otherwise why would they be binding him like that? 'Less'n they were going to pitch him into the river to

116

drown.' Then they carried Pete into his own house and came out again at once, so that wasn't the game.

One of the problems with living outside the law, as the brothers Frobisher had done for several years, was that there was nobody to whom you could appeal in cases such as the present one. All that Jake could do was watch and wait, hoping that no harm would befall his brother.

The journey to the Rio Grande was horribly slow and there wasn't one of the men, including Quinnell and Bob Wheeler, who didn't wonder at some point what they would do if a US cavalry patrol showed up and asked them what they had in their cart. They had scattered a little brushwood over the rifles but it was a mighty thin disguise. Anybody walking up close to that wagon would be sure to see at once that it was stacked with weaponry.

As they plodded along the road south Captain Quinnell talked matters over with Wheeler.

'You know the Frobishers?' he asked.

'Never met 'em,' said Wheeler, 'but I heard as they're straight dealers. How's it goin' to work with the money? You ain't sending the guns across the river and then relying on the honesty of Juarez's men?'

Quinnell laughed out loud at that.

'How long you known me, Bob?' he said. 'No, That's not what I'm planning. They're sending a couple of boys 'cross the river and some of them will be on the other bank as well. Any sign of double dealing and them and us both'll be facing a blood-bath. Don't think they want that any more than we do.'

Bob Wheeler grunted.

'You're certain-sure that we all of us are goin' to get this free land as Maximilian is handing out?' he asked. 'You ain't a fixin' up for to run some plantation with me and the others as overseers or somethin' of that sort?'

'We been through a heap together, Bob, over the last four years. I like you well enough, but I wouldn't cross you, not for a king's ransom. You rest easy on that point.'

'Wouldn't cross me, hey? That your famous honour or what?'

'Honour don't enter into the equation,' said Quinnell with a chuckle. 'I know that if I tried to cheat you you'd come after me with murder in your heart. I reckon you might succeed in the endeavour, what's more.'

It was Bob Wheeler's turn to laugh aloud.

'I reckon that you and me understand each other all right, Captain.'

When Quinnell's band were about three miles from the river the captain called a halt. They were passing through a sparse little pine wood and, although they could just catch a glimpse of the Rio Grande between the trees, it was unlikely that anybody sitting on the bank would be able to see them.

'What's to do?' said Wheeler. 'Why've we stopped?'

118

'You ever have the feeling during the late war,' asked Quinnell, 'like a prickling at the back of your neck? That little tickling that means danger is near at hand?'

'I mind well enough what you're talkin' of. You think we're riding into a trap?'

'I couldn't rightly say,' answered the captain, rubbing his chin thoughtfully, 'but something doesn't feel right.'

'That's good enough for me,' declared Wheeler at once. 'I never yet knew you to be led astray by your senses. What d'you want to do?'

'It would ease my mind greatly if somebody were to ride out alone to that landing and then trot along the road west a ways. Just make out as he was an ordinary traveller, with no special interest in the Frobishers' sct-up. You hear what I say?'

'Sure. You want me to go or do we ask one of the other boys?'

Quinnell and Wheeler were talking softly a little way off from the others so that they could not be heard.

'I'd sooner trust your report than that of any of the others,' Quinnell said. 'If you'd go I'd rest easier for knowing that nothing would have been missed.'

Bob Wheeler nodded thoughtfully. For all that he got a little irritated with the captain from time to time they understood and trusted each other's judgement perfectly, at least in matters such as this.

He trotted his horse around and headed off to the left, aiming to break cover from the woods at some little distance from where the others waited. He wanted to be sure that if anybody hostile was watching from the river they would see only him and not catch a glimpse of the wagon and the riders surrounding it. When he emerged from the wood Wheeler rode at a sedate trot to the road, which ran from east to west more or less alongside the river. On reaching the road he turned to the west and rode in the general direction of El Paso.

Wheeler knew roughly what the set-up was with the Frobishers and that they lived on opposite banks of the river. As he approached the little stone-built hut he saw that there was a similar structure on the Mexican side of the Rio Grande. This was the place, he'd bet on it. The only snag was that there was no sign of any white American near the hut, just a bunch of Mexicans some of who looked to be natives. They cast incurious glances at him as he rode past.

'Good day to you!' called Bob Wheeler as he trotted past, but none of the men replied. He carried on down the road. When he glanced back ten minutes later he found that he was out of sight of the men by the river, so he veered to the right, rode back to the wood and rejoined the others.

CHAPTER 9

As the rider disappeared along the road Sergeant Carlos spoke to the colonel.

'I'll be bound that you recognize that one, sir?'

'It is rarely enough that a man plants his boot on my buttocks,' replied Lopez, a thin smile on his face. 'I am not apt to forget the man who takes such a liberty with my person. How do you read his presence here, Carlos? Coincidence or otherwise?'

'Hardly coincidence.'

'So I would suppose. I shall speak a few words with our captive, I think.'

Pete Frobisher's heart had began to pound when two of the Mexicans entered his house and one of them, without saying a word, hauled him to his feet. Was this the end of the road for him? Despite their assurances, were these fellows about to cut his throat?

'My colonel would ask you some questions,' said the man who had dragged him to his feet.

'Mr Frobisher,' said the other, 'We know that a group of Confederates are bringing guns here for you to send across the river into Mexico.'

Pete Frobisher began babbling indignant noises, indicative of innocence, but the man standing in front of him said gently:

'No, we don't have time to listen to your foolish lies. If shooting starts you are as likely to die as any of us. Your only hope is to be honest about this.'

'I mind now that something was arranged about such a thing,' admitted Frobisher reluctantly. 'Fellow with a Southern accent did come by here to fix up an arrangement of the sort.'

'How was the matter to be conducted?'

'I was to let my brother know when they was due and he would go off and find those as was to purchase the weapons.'

'How would you tell your brother that the men were here?'

'We use flags. Semaphore signals.'

'You can do so now?'

'Could do, I reckon.'

Frobisher's mind was working furiously. It was a thousand to one against any of these boys knowing how to read the flags, so he could say pretty much anything he pleased to Jake. Only thing was, he hardly knew what he should say. This polite and well-spoken foreigner was perfectly right in saying that if there was to be a gun battle, then Pete himself would be as likely to die as anybody else.

'What would you have me tell my brother?' he

asked, playing for time.

'Only the truth: that the men with the rifles are arriving. Nothing more.'

Try as he might, Pete couldn't think of any edge that he could gain by deceiving these men in passing a secret message to his brother. He certainly didn't want the law coming down here, nor the army either, if it came to the matter of that. The best he and Jake could hope was that they could weather this latest storm, then slip out of this area and start afresh elsewhere. The game wasn't worth the candle any more.

'I'll tell my brother what you want,' he said. 'You still aim to leave me with my life?'

The reply was all the more chilling for the casual and courteous way in which it was delivered. The Mexican looked at Pete and then said in faultless English:

'I can't think of any advantage to me in your death, Mr Frobisher, and so I shall leave you alive. If things should change and I decide to kill you, then I promise that I'll give you enough warning to say your prayers and so on.'

When Bob Wheeler returned to the waiting band of men they were expecting him to tell them that there was nothing to worry about: that they could just ride forward now. Instead he said:

'Looks like we got a problem. . . .'

After Wheeler had outlined what he had seen at the river the men talked among themselves, trying to figure out what was the best thing to do. Some thought that the men Wheeler had seen might have been Juarez's men, waiting for them, while others, a little more shrewdly, guessed that the men were from the Mexican army and were intending to put a stop to gun-running across the border at that point.

Finally, when they'd talked themselves dry, they turned to the captain, to hear what he might have to say about the subject.

Quinnell had already decided that they should treat those holding that part of the riverbank as hostiles. There was no reason at all why the rebels should go to the trouble of ferrying a dozen men over on that rope. The likelihood was that these men had been sent by the army to interfere in his, Quinnell's, business, and that was a ploy that Barnabas Quinnell did not intend to countenance in any way.

'Here's how the land lies,' he said. 'I don't think for a minute that those boys Bob here saw are the ones wanting to buy our Henrys. Why would they send a dozen men across the river for that? No, I think it more likely that these are agents of the Emperor, waiting to ambush us if we show up with our cargo.'

'What're we to do then?' asked somebody. 'We're running powerful low on cash money. If we don't sell these damned rifles I don't know how we'll get by 'til we're paid.'

There were murmurs of agreement at this.

'Don't start fretting,' said the captain. 'Those

weapons will bring in a good price once we get them over the border. I was hoping that we could sell them here and get the money without being burdened with them when we actually cross into Mexico. Seems it's not to be.

'Here's what we can do instead. You know that after we'd conducted our little bit of business with those fellows who run that smuggling operation we were going to make our way down to the ferry, along the way to El Paso?

'All we do now is carry on and take that ferry anyway, with the wagon and all. It won't take long to make contact with the rebels and we'll sell the rifles in Mexico. Probably get more for them there than we would have here. Five dollars each was mighty cheap.'

Such was the men's trust in Captain Quinnell that there was no grumbling about this sudden change of plan.

Quinnell would have liked to have gone down to the crossing there and then, to wipe out those bastards who had queered his pitch, but he didn't think that there would be a whole heap of enthusiasm for such a pointless and unnecessary piece of bloodshed; not when they were so close to their goal. Bob Wheeler cleared up this point by asking:

'We're just goin' to pass along the road peaceable like, is that the score? Let that ferry take us over the Rio Grande, dispose of our goods and then ride down to New Virginia?'

Captain Quinnell felt a momentary spasm of irritation on finding himself backed into a definite position in this way, but he recovered himself sufficiently to smile.

'Sure, that's what I had in mind,' he replied.

As is so often the case with momentous events, everything was now upset by the most trivial of causes.

'We can't take this here cart through the wood,' one of the men pointed out, 'if we're intending to avoid the men at that crossing. It'd overturn for sure on some tree root. It's bad enough keeping it steady and on an even keel on a level road, never mind about trying to get it over a rough patch of woodland.'

This was indubitably true and, now that they thought on the matter, it was clear that the only way to get that wagon down to where the ferry was operating would be to follow the track through the wood until it joined the road running alongside the river.

There was nothing for it but to ride right past the men who had control of the smugglers' crossing.

'So be it,' said Captain Quinnell. 'Let's move out. With luck we might reach the ferry before dark.'

The situation was, as they all knew deep inside themselves, far from ideal. The whole purpose of using the two brothers and their set-up had been to avoid questions about what they might be carrying in the cart.

In the usual way of things the ferry, which was little more than a raft pulled by ropes from one bank

126

of the Rio Grande to the other, was nothing to worry about. The man who ran it was incurious and they might have been transporting twelve-pounder artillery pieces for all that he would be likely to care about it.

Times were not normal though, right now, and both Quinnell and Bob Wheeler were wondering whether they would find either Yankee soldiers on this bank or some of Maximilian's men on the other, charged with keeping a friendly and benevolent eye upon the goods being ferried from one country to the other. It was a damned nuisance.

As it happened, Quinnell and his little band were destined never to reach the ferry, so the matter was not put to the test.

Once they started along the track leading to the river a couple of the men, for no special reason, began singing 'The Bonny Blue Flag'. It seemed somehow fitting. They would, after all, be leaving their own country behind soon; if not for ever then surely for a good, long spell. Why not sing a last chorus of the old song?

The men guarding the river crossing could hear snatches of song as the wagon and riders approached them.

'*Hurrah for the bonny blue flag that bears a single star!*' and '*For Southern rights, hurrah!*'

Colonel Lopez was the only one among the Mexicans whose English was good enough to understand the words, and he found that his heart was hardened against these rascally Southerners.

Southern rights? What did that mean, but the 'right' to keep slaves and make beasts of burden of their fellow men?

Until the very moment that he heard those words Lopez had not been finally decided as to the course of action that he would pursue. Now though, listening to those wretches boasting of the odious way of life in which they had revelled before the War Between the States and thinking that they were going to start the same kind of arrangement in Lopez's own country by exploiting his fellow countrymen as they had previously used the Negroes, Lopez thought to himself: It isn't to be borne!

It was a strangely satisfying situation, because the colonel found that his duty to the Emperor Maximilian, his personal loyalty to Juarez and the desire to be revenged upon the man who had kicked him to the ground, all coincided in perfect harmony.

He had promised to make an example of some of the gunrunners so as to discourage the rest. Shooting these devils would accomplish that end. He was opposed to the idea of the foreign colonies being established in his country; killing these men would work towards that aim.

Finally, he had a score to settle with the men who had mocked and humiliated him in the saloon at Pike's Landing. Burning down the saloon had satisfied part of that debt, but shooting the men concerned would finish the job neatly.

'Carlos,' said the colonel, 'what do you say we do now?'

'Do, sir?' asked his sergeant in amazement. 'Why, I say we should kill every one of these sons of whores with no further delay.'

'Once more, my old comrade, our minds run along similar grooves. Give the order to prepare.'

The men had already assembled their carbines in readiness and the weapons were now loaded, primed and ready to fire. The wagon and its accompanying riders were only a hundred yards away, riding along the road towards them with no sign at all that they were apprehensive of any danger.

Lopez knew that he would not be able to give the order to fire without at least challenging these men. It would be cold-blooded murder to shoot at them unawares. Carlos apparently had no such scruples about the matter.

'Cock your pieces and prepare to fire at the advancing troops,' he said to the soldiers. There sounded a dozen metallic clicks as the men pulled back the hammers with their thumbs and sighted down the barrels at the oncoming riders.

'Do not fire until I give the command,' said Lopez suddenly. 'Hold fast.'

'Those boys are drawing down on us,' said Bob Wheeler in a casual voice, as if he had noticed rain clouds coming in from the west. 'I say we should rein in and parley.'

'Halt!' cried Captain Quinnell. 'Not a step further.'

The riders and cart came to a halt with jingling of harness and one or two oaths from the men themselves. They were no more than fifty yards from Lopez's men standing to the left of the road. Quinnell's men hadn't drawn their weapons, partly because they were waiting for the order from the captain but also because they all knew that a ferocious gun battle was now a real possibility and the very act of pulling a pistol could be enough to spark off a bloody massacre.

'I don't rightly know who you folk might be,' called Quinnell to the Mexicans, 'but we have no quarrel with you. Will you hold the road against us?'

'As to that,' Colonel Lopez shouted back, 'tell us first what you have in your wagon.'

'None of your damned business. We're getting restless here. Will you let us pass or do you want to fight?'

'We'll search you for a consigment of weapons. Then you can be on your way.'

The sheer audacity of this proposal took away the breath of the men accompanying the wagonload of rifles. Shielded by the wagon from the view of the Mexicans standing ahead of them with their rifles trained upon them, Bob Wheeler very slowly withdrew the Whitworth from its long scabbard, which was attached to his saddle. He moved with infinite delicacy, keeping his head raised, and not giving any indication that he was doing anything hostile. The wagon blocked any view of his hands and he was able to extract the rifle, cock it and prepare to raise it to his shoulder. It was not difficult to gauge that the spokesman of the waylaying group, who was now bandying words with the captain, was the leader of the men who wished to examine their luggage.

During the war Sergeant Wheeler had always found that if there was to be any shooting the sooner it was done with and out of the way the better. He had also learned that there was generally an advantage in being the first side to start shooting. Men under fire seldom fire as calmly and accurately as those not in that position.

It looked as though an impasse had been reached, with the men covering the riders still keeping their guns trained on their targets, and those escorting the wagon showing not the least inclination to submit to an inspection of the goods that they were transporting along the road.

Something had to give and it was Bob Wheeler who lit the match that set off the powder keg. He was gripping his rifle with both hands, keeping it so low that nobody ahead could have seen that was holding it.

Between him and his intended target was the wagonload of rifles and three of their own men, including Captain Quinnell. It would have to be the best shot of his whole life. Before bringing his weapon to bear Wheeler rehearsed the move mentally, until he felt that he could raise his piece and get off a shot before anybody had time to guess what he was about.

Wheeler's gambit so very nearly came off. He raised the Whitworth to his shoulder, sighted down the telescope and fired, all in the merest fraction of a second. Captain Quinnell heard the heavy-calibre bullet fizz past his head like like an angry hornet. The sound of the shot followed almost immediately.

Fortunately for Lopez he had expected something of the sort and had been peering intently ahead, trying to calculate which of the Anglos would be the first to fire. He glimpsed a movement over the shoulder of the man who had been negotiating on behalf of the Confederates, and he ducked instinctively. Consequently the ball flew over his head. It buried itself in the man standing behind him, striking his throat and then driving down at an angle and rupturing his heart. Luis Gortari dropped dead on the spot.

Then all became a brief hell as the two bands of men were engulfed in crashing gunfire and acrid smoke. The shooting lasted only thirty seconds or so, before faltering to a halt. Quinnell had been killed almost at once, most of the Mexicans having already been aiming at him as he spoke.

He fell from his horse with three balls embedded in his head and chest; he had not even had the opportunity to draw his own weapon. Bob Wheeler dismounted as soon as he had fired at Colonel Lopez. He set the Whitworth down on the ground once he was off his horse. It was a muzzle-loader and Wheeler had a strong suspicion that this fight was not going to last long enough for anybody to have the chance to reload such a piece.

The chief aim of an engagement like this was to throw as much lead towards the enemy as could be achieved in the shortest possible time. He accordingly drew both the pistols that flapped against his hips and began shooting more or less randomly in the direction of those he conceived to be the enemy: the men who had challenged them.

Sergeant Carlos had the most keenly developed sense of danger and had dropped to the ground before the first bullet came buzzing towards them. He was as deadly a shot with his pistol at fifty yards as most men would be with a hunting rifle. He had taken two of the Anglos out before they realized what was happening. In fact Bob Wheeler's first shot took his own side more by surprise than it did his enemies. This accounted for the fact that the Confederates came off considerably worse in the brief firefight than did the Mexicans.

When the smoke had cleared all but two of the Americans were lying either dead or grievously wounded. For their part, the Mexican soldiers had lost only three men killed and two others badly but not mortally injured.

It was as plain as a pikestaff to Bob Wheeler that his friends were nigh-on all dead and that if he lingered any longer in the vicinity he was likely to join them. Ignoring the other survivor of the battle, a man he had never really cared for overmuch, Wheeler leaped on to his horse and rode as fast as he could back to the wood. One or two desultory shots were sent in his direction, but none came anywhere near him.

The other surviving member of the band was not as swift or lucky as Wheeler. When he saw the former sergeant galloping away Jack Trotter hesitated for a moment and glanced nervously towards the river. In the time that it took him to make up his mind that he too intended to flee from the field of battle, one of the Mexican soldiers, who had now had ample time to reload, took careful aim and shot Trotter, causing him to fall from his horse.

The aftermath of even a small military engagement is a melancholy affair and although the Mexicans had 'won', there were still three of their comrades lying dead upon the dusty ground. Lopez and Sergeant Carlos went over to where the wagon stood, surrounded now by dead and dying men and horses. Carlos put two wounded animals out of their misery with pistol shots through their brains, while the colonel went to see if anything could be done for the wounded men. He soon saw that it was hopeless.

There were three living men from the Confederate band. Only one of these was conscious and, judging by the rapid, shallow breathing, would not last more than a few minutes more. The other two men also seemed to Lopez to be at the point of death; since they had both passed out from pain or loss of blood there was little that could be done to aid them.

Before any care was lavished upon any of his

fallen foes Colonel Lopez took the precaution of removing any deadly weapons from their reach. Compassion was a fine, Christian virtue but he had no desire to be assassinated by a dying man: one who might be desperate for company in his journey to the next world.

CHAPTER 10

The last of the men to be wounded by the Mexican gunfire lay on his back in a pitiful attitude suggestive of agonizing pain. Jack Trotter was only a young man; he had been just seventeen years of age when the war began and was still a few months short of his twenty-first birthday.

A quick look at him showed that the ball had entered his back but had not exited. Judging from the frothy, bright crimson blood that dribbled from his mouth, Colonel Lopez deduced it to be probable that the bullet had lodged in one of the man's lungs and that his life expectancy was a matter of minutes rather than hours or days.

'I am sorry that you have come to such a pass,' said Lopez gently. 'I fear that it is all up with you now. Would you like me to pray with you?'

The dying young man smiled and then grimaced in pain.

'Never been much of a one for prayer, to tell the truth. I could surely do with a smoke though.'

The colonel reached into the bag on his back and extracted a flat cigar case. He looked inside.

'You are in luck, my young friend,' he said. 'I have just one left.'

'Ain't I the lucky one though?' said the man, trying once more to flash a devil-may-care smile. Lopez lit the thin cigar and placed it between the wounded Confederate's lips. The young man drew in the smoke greedily.

They remained in this position for a few minutes, the man stretched out upon the ground and Lopez squatting at his side, until there was a slight groan and the cigar dropped from the fellow's lips. Colonel Lopez picked it up and then felt for a pulse. There was none.

Carlos had finished now with his own business. He had disposed humanely of those beasts that were already dying and checked over the others. Only two of the horses had sustained no injury.

'What now?' asked Sergeant Carlos. The colonel stood up.

'We render these rifles useless and leave them here, as a reminder to show everybody why these men died. Then, I think, I shall have have fulfilled the Emperor's instructions to the very letter. If I choose after that to leave his Imperial Majesty's service, then I may do so with my honour intact and unblemished.'

Carlos, whose upbringing had been a little less genteel than his superior officer's, thought privately that this was all a lot of nonsense. Honour! What value was there in this strange and intangible commodity? Could you eat or drink it? Did it keep you warm at night? Could it be sold in the market at a profit? From all that he was able to apprehend, this 'honour' of the colonel's was a confounded nuisance! Nevertheless he kept his own counsel and said merely:

'Just as you say, sir. What shall we do with the guns? Is it truly necessary to destroy them all? Could we not take a few with us? If,' he added hastily, 'if, that is, we are going to join His Excellency.'

Colonel Lopez gave his subordinate an inscrutable look.

'I have not yet made my plans,' he replied. 'It is enough for now that I fulfill the orders that I received as a colonel of the Imperial army. We shall dispose of every one of these rifles. I think a fire will do the trick. Once the wooden stocks are burning and the fire is hot enough, the mechanisms will be damaged too.'

Sergeant Carlos saluted, turned to do as he had been ordered. Then he fell dead with a bullet through his brain. It happened so quickly that even after his old comrade had dropped to the ground, a gout of blood pouring from the side of his head, Lopez just stood there, staring stupidly.

In the pine wood Bob Wheeler was congratulating himself on what could easily prove to be the best shot of his life. The Mexican had been fully 1,200 yards away and yet he had taken him out with a perfectly judged head shot. If only there could have been somebody to appreciate such a fine piece of marksmanship.

There was no time to dally, though, to savour his achievement, because the other Mexicans were now running to the fallen man and scanning the woods to see if they could spot any clue as to the whereabouts of the sniper. It was time to be off. Wheeler went over to his mount and replaced the Whitworth in its scabbard before hoisting himself into the saddle and cantering away from the scene of his latest conquest.

All things considered, Bob Wheeler felt that he had escaped lightly enough from this latest complication. It was true that every one of his friends and companions had been slaughtered, but it was also the fact that he himself was still in the land of the living. That was a great consolation. He had enough information about the settlement of New Virginia to be tolerably sure of finding his way there alone, and of being able to sell his talents to the Imperial Mexican Army. From all that he could make out, the Emperor Maximilian and his boys were just falling over themselves to hand out parcels of land to former Confederates like him. He would make out well enough, even without the captain's help.

Wheeler had decided some time since that a parting of the ways between him and Captain Quinnell was pretty much inevitable, and in some ways he was glad that it had happened so neatly and with so little inconvenience to himself. He had his life, his horse and his guns. What more could a man ask?

All that remained, before he made his way downstream to the ferry, was to wipe out those interfering devils who had queered his pitch so badly. Because if there was one thing Wheeler couldn't abide at any price it was folk as couldn't tend to their own affairs and leave him to mind his. He was a man who knew how to carry a grudge and before he dug up and headed south to New Virginia, he was damned if he wasn't going to kill every mother's son of those cursed men who had seized the Henrys from the Confederate band.

By the time the Mexicans reached the tree line there was no sign of the man who had shot Carlos. They drifted back, trying to ignore the astonishing and embarrassing sight of the famous Colonel Lopez weeping like child over the loss of his brave and faithful servant.

Pete Frobisher heard the brief flurry of shots, though he had no idea who had come out on top in the fight. Perhaps a little less than a half-hour after the gun battle the door to his house was opened and in walked the man who had spoken such flawless English. This man addressed him thus:

'We are almost ready to leave you to your own devices, sir. I understand that you have a sling or seat or some such conveyance, which will enable a man to cross the river. Is it not so?'

'I don't advertise it overmuch,' said Frobisher,

'but yes, me and my brother's got something of the kind. You sure you ain't about to make an end of me, to rid yourselves of witnesses, as it might be?'

'Nothing of the kind,' said Colonel Lopez. 'Once we cross the Rio Grande you will not set eyes on us again.'

'What a mercy that'll be!' muttered Pete Frobisher softly. 'You untie me now and I'll signal to my brother and get things moving. I'll warrant you're all as anxious to be clear of here as I am to see you gone.'

'Doubtless that is true. One of my men will free you.'

It had seemed wise to the colonel not to set fire to the rifles and ammunition until they were ready to cross the border back into Mexico. It was to be hoped that the shooting had not already attracted the attention of any army patrol; it would be sheer madness to set fire to a wagonload of guns and powder and not expect somebody to spot the resulting smoke. The last complication that anybody would wish at this stage was a cavalry patrol riding down upon them to investigate what might be happening.

Little reason as the cavalry might have to love the men who had stolen those rifles, they would be even less well disposed towards foreign soldiers, operating in civilian clothing and massacring American citizens. No, torching the wagon would be the final act of the tragedy; not to be undertaken until they were all on the point of crossing back into Mexico.

141

It was a genuine grief to Colonel Lopez that Carlos had been killed, but he knew that he would be compelled to put off any mourning until a more convenient season. His duty now lay with the living; he had six men, two of them very badly injured, to see safely back into their own country.

Every minute that passed increased the danger of somebody riding by, quite by chance, and finding dead bodies lying all over the road. It was now that Pete Frobisher announced an unlooked for difficulty. His brother had gone off somewhere and Pete had not the least notion of where that somewhere might be, nor yet when Jake was likely to return.

'It's not like old Jake,' said Frobisher apologetically. 'I reckon as the gunfire might o' spooked him.'

'Can you not fix up the line without your brother's assistance?' asked Colonel Lopez with superhuman patience. 'The case is urgent.'

'Not hardly,' said Frobisher. 'Has to be secured to that tall oak on his side o' the river. Else the pulley won't work, see?'

'What then do you recommend?' asked Lopez through gritted teeth.

'Happen we'll have to wait 'til Jake gets back.'

There was nothing for it but to go along with this suggestion. The colonel made sure that the men gathered everything together so that when the time came to cross there would be no delay. Other than that there was little to be done. Not the least of his regrets was that he would be obliged to leave Carlos's body here. It was unthinkable to start carting a

142

corpse around with him, especially since they would need to move as swiftly as could be when the time came.

All that remained possible to do was to sit and wait. This circumstance was very far from satisfying as far as Pete Frobisher was concerned.

'I don't suppose you boys'd mind moving away from my house, would you?' he said to the colonel. 'With all them corpses lying round and me and Jake's rope and so on, I'm afeared that if anybody comes by here it's going to look like I'm mixed up in some funny business.'

Lopez, who was still struggling to maintain his equanimity after the the death of Sergeant Carlos, gave the smuggler a baleful look.

'We've let you stay alive so far,' he replied, 'which is more than some men in our position might have done. Do not make me repent of promising not to kill you.'

Pete Frobisher knew when it was time to hold his tongue, so he wandered off, muttering to himself. At the next moment he caught sight of Jake, riding down to his side of the river.

'Thank Christ for that!' exclaimed Frobisher, hurrying off to fetch his signalling flags.

The conversation with his brother was watched closely by the Mexicans including Lopez, who gave Pete Frobisher the creeps. After asking Jake to raise the rope at his end and prepare to transport a half-dozen men across the river, Pete ventured to enquire where the Sam Hill his brother had just taken off to.

Jake's reply was not altogether to Pete's liking, for his brother told him that he had been off to talk to the rebels, to let them know that the rifles they'd been expecting had been intercepted and that some men were now about to cross the river who might not be well disposed towards them.

'You jackass!' signalled Pete Frobisher in an agitated fashion. 'You want to get caught up in another battle? I surely don't!'

The semaphore exchange had been going on for longer than Colonel Lopez liked. He spoke to Frobisher.

'You and your brother have a lot to say to each other,' he said. 'You wouldn't be plotting treachery, I suppose? If so, I can promise you that either you or your brother – and most likely both of you – will die this day.'

'Lordy, but you are a s-suspicious fellow!' stuttered Frobisher. 'I'm just fixing up with my brother Jake about how to carry the wounded men across, without them falling in the Rio Grande. Only thinking of your own best interests, see?'

Lopez eyed the man coldly and spoke once again.

'Play us false and you will be dead before nightfall.'

After the two brothers had communicated with each other they busied themselves with hauling up the rope from where it lay on the riverbed. This was quite a tricky procedure and Lopez thought it best just to leave the brothers to get on with it.

Bob Wheeler fully intended to ride on down to

GUNS ACROSS THE RIO GRANDE

the ferry and cross over the border as soon as he might, but he was damned if he would let anybody put one over on him like this, killing his companions and depriving him of $200 which he had thought were as good as in his pocket. His self-respect would by no means allow such liberties to be taken with him or those associated with him. He would have to even up the score before leaving.

After riding deeper into the wood to evade the men who had come searching for him after he'd let fly with the Whitworth, Wheeler circled around until he had come back to where the trees petered out and he had a fine view of the river.

There looked to be six or seven men milling round the house of that fellow who'd promised to take the rifles over the water for them. Were those fellows planning to sell the Henrys on their own account? From where he was crouching Wheeler could see that the wagon stood where it had been during the shoot-out; the men had made no attempt to shift the cargo down to the riverside.

This suggested that their aim had not been to seize the guns for their own profit but, more likely, just to screw up the operation and prevent the guns getting over into Mexico. It took no great leap of the intellect to deduce from this that the men who had opposed them must be agents of the Mexican government; fellows charged with disrupting the gun-running across the border.

While he was figuring all this out Wheeler noticed that the two men who lived on opposite banks of the river were hauling up the rope that they used to transport goods from one side to the other. There was no sign of anybody fetching the rifles, so it was a fair guess that the aim was to take the men who had attacked them back to their own side of the border.

Well, thought Wheeler to himself, we'll just see about that; one bad turn deserves another!

Leaving his horse tethered in the wood, Wheeler waited until the men by the river were all staring across to the other bank, watching while the fellow there raised the rope, secured it to a tree and then sprinted across the open ground towards the wagonload of arms. When he was about halfway there Wheeler dropped to the ground, satisfied that he was unlikely to be seen by the men he was stalking.

While Wheeler was wriggling his way slowly and patiently across the straggly grass towards the cart, Colonel Lopez was discussing the best way to get the wounded men across the river. Pete Frobisher showed him the sling that he had in the past used to pass men above the foaming surface of the Rio Grande. It was essentially no more than an old harness from a draught horse, with a pulley wheel attached to the top. The passenger sat in the hoop and was then pulled along the rope by whichever of the brothers was on the opposite bank.

'Are you sure that it is strong enough?' asked Lopez doubtfully. 'It will take the weight of a man?'

'Nobody fall into the water yet,' said Frobisher. 'In any case, that's all there is. You don't like it, then you can try your luck downstream at the ferry.'

146

'Do not adopt that tone with me,' said the colonel in a deadly voice, 'You wish to live, then be a little more agreeable.'

Pete Frobisher shrugged. He was reasonably confident now that this well-spoken foreigner was not the kind to see a man shot out of hand.

'It's all we got, my brother and me,' he said in a slightly more polite tone of voice. 'It's worked well enough up to now.'

Lopez went over to the most badly wounded of his men.

'I know that your collar bone is shattered,' he said quietly. 'You are in pain. The only way across the river is to sit in that sling and hang on. We must go soon, the Anglos are liable to hang us on the spot if we're caught here, you comprehend?'

'I can do it, sir,' replied the man. 'I can hold fast with my left hand.'

'Good man,' said Lopez approvingly. He turned to the other soldier with a serious injury. This man had taken a ball through his leg and was accordingly bleeding like a stuck pig.

'What of you, my friend?' Lopez asked. 'You have lost a lot of blood. You are not too weak to make the crossing?'

'I shall manage,' declared the soldier stoutly.

It was decided that the wounded men should cross first and everybody gathered at the waterside to watch anxiously as the men were pulled slowly along the rope. The rope sagged so low that when the men were exactly halfway across their feet were dangling only a few inches above the water.

While the Mexicans were messing around with their evacuation Bob Wheeler thought that he could risk rising to his feet and running to the wagon. Not one of the fools turned round while he was doing this. If Jake Frobisher, who was staring in Wheeler's direction the whole time, did see him, then he didn't feel called upon to mention the fact to the men he was drawing across the water on the improvised sling.

Once the two injured men were over safely Colonel Lopez spoke to the remaining men.

'Now we must move with even more haste,' he told them. 'Two of you go and set fire to that wagon and its contents. The other two can make their way over the river. Hurry now.'

All four of the men saluted. After a few brief words among themselves two went over to where Pete Frobisher was standing; the others began collecting brushwood with a view to burning the rifles. As one of the men was hoisting himself into the sling the two who were to set fire to the wagon walked towards it, carrying armfuls of dry wood and desiccated weeds.

They were only a few feet away when Bob Wheeler leaped up with a pistol in his hand. Burdened as they were with kindling, neither man was able to get to his gun in a hurry. Wheeler killed them both, needing only one shot for each.

The sound of shots from the direction of the wagon took Colonel Lopez entirely by surprise. At first he wondered if one of the injured Confederates might have rallied sufficiently to start shooting, but then he recalled that he had removed all the weapons from the wounded. It took only another second's thought to tell Lopez that this must be the work of the fellow who had shot Carlos.

There was only one man left standing at Lopez's side. The other was almost at the Mexican side of the river; once the sling had been sent back it would only take a few minutes for this fellow too to be pulled to safety. All arguments of reason, as well as sound military strategy, suggested that Colonel Lopez should simply abandon his position now and make his own way across the rope to the Mexican shore.

Doing so, though, would leave those rifles in the hands of hostile forces and Lopez had sworn to dispose of them. He could not just give up his quest now. Only when he had finished to his own satisfaction the task that the Emperor had requested him to undertake would Colonel Lopez be free: free to change, if he wished, his allegiance.

With a heavy heart Lopez spoke to the young soldier at his side.

'Leave me your rifle, my young friend,' he said. 'I have a little business to conduct here before I too leave the United States.'

CHAPTER 11

Having dealt neatly and expeditiously with the two men who had approached his hiding-place, Wheeler now waited for the leader of their group who, he assumed, would now tackle him. He didn't really know why he thought that this would be the case, it was just a strange feeling that he had.

He reloaded the two empty chambers in his pistol and then brought the Whitworth to bear on the scene at the river crossing. There were now two men standing by the rope on this side; a third was about to land on the Mexican shore. He peered down the brass telescope and took very careful aim. Then Bob Wheeler squeezed the trigger gently.

The fact that the young soldier had just reached the riverbank and was swinging himself from the makeshift hoist saved his life. Wheeler was using the sniper's rifle well within its range and, in the usual way of things, should have been able to hit a stationary target; after all, the man at whom he was aiming was only about a quarter of a mile from him.

Things were not as he might have hoped, though. For one thing a stiff breeze had blown up; for another, his target was moving, swinging back and forth from the rope as the young man tried to gain purchase with his feet and scramble down from the sling.

The ball hit the bank a few inches from where Jake Frobisher was standing. For a moment he wondered what it was that had caused the earth to erupt like that near his foot. He thought at first that it was some little burrowing animal emerging from the ground; then came the sound of a distant shot. Realizing that he was under fire, Frobisher dived for cover.

Across the river Colonel Lopez's suspicions were confirmed; he knew that a lone gunman was hiding behind that cart of rifles and ammunition. It would be madness for him and the remaining man to try and get over the river with that fellow taking pot shots at them.

On the other hand, it would be equally suicidal to charge the position. He would be shot down before he was a hundred yards from the cart. Even staying where he was was not a practical option. It was surely only a matter of time before some cavalry patrol passed by and he and this young man were both captured.

There was one faint chance, but since it was the only one there was no choice but to attempt it. Lopez spoke to the soldier.

'Tell me truly now, are you a good shot?' he asked.

151

The boy, for he was little more than that, shook his head.

'To speak in truth sir, I am not,' he replied.

'That is what I feared. Listen, we must both get behind the house here. Whoever is firing at us has a good weapon and we are within his range.'

They had taken only a few steps before Pete Frobisher caught sight of them.

'Where are you two scuttling off to now?' he demanded to know. 'Me and my brother would be obliged if you could just finish this business as quick as you like. This is getting a mite too lively for me, I'll tell you that for nothing!'

'I must ask you to bear with us for a minute or two, Mr Frobisher,' replied the colonel. 'There is one small matter that requires my attention.'

'Well, make it snappy, hey?' replied Frobisher irritably.

Although he was far from being an exceptional shot, Colonel Lopez had the germ of an idea that, he thought, might yet save the day. He picked up one of the Sharps carbines left behind by the wounded men and hefted it in his hand. It was loaded.

He went to the corner of Frobisher's house; its sturdy stone wall would provide good cover. His edge came from the fact that he had examined the material in the wagon and had noted the disposition of the various supplies. In particular he had noticed two cardboard boxes labelled Caps. These would each contain 500 copper percussion caps, which fitted over the nipples of muzzle-loading weapons.

The inside of each of these caps was smeared with a generous dollop of fulminate of mercury, a sensitive explosive that was detonated by the impact of the gun's hammer falling.

Kneeling like the infantryman he had once been, Lopez sighted down the barrel and took aim at the wagon. It was something over 200 yards to the wagon and he wondered whether the Sharps would be accurate enough at such a distance.

There was only one way to find out; he loosed off a shot at the load on the cart. His first ball was a little low, striking and splintering a spoke of the wheel. That was the only fault though; he had fallen short of his target. The aim had been true enough in that he had not struck to the left or right of the point at which he had aimed.

Lopez was not given much time to congratulate himself on his marksmanship, because no sooner had his own ball struck the wagon's wheel than a bullet came flying in his direction. Obviously, the sniper was still hiding behind the wagon. Rather than waste time reloading the colonel took the rifle of the other wounded man and again took aim. He felt that he had the range and he elevated the barrel, just a shade, to compensate for the range. This time the effect was all that could have been hoped.

The .5-calibre ball, weighing 600 grains, sped towards the wagon at 1,400 feet per second. It ploughed straight into one of the cardboard boxes containing the percussion caps. Distributed throughout the several hundred copper caps in this box was an amount in the region of two ounces of fulminate of mercury. Such was the force of the ball as it struck home that half the caps exploded on its impact, instantly setting off the other half in the box. The exploding of the contents of this first box then detonated the caps in the box above.

A total of four ounces of high explosive thus went off, causing the thirty pounds of fine-grained black powder also to go up. The effect of all this was as though two fifteen-pound artillery shells had landed right on top of the cart and exploded.

The massive blast turned the cart and its load to a pile of matchwood and tangled metal. A vast plume of black smoke rose from the site of the explosion; even at that distance Colonel Lopez felt a wave of warm air flow past him. The boom echoed to and fro; it must surely have been audible for miles. The young soldier who had been sheltering with Lopez behind the walls of Frobisher's home stood up and peered round the corner.

'Mother of God!' he exclaimed. 'I think you have settled all accounts now, sir.'

Pete Frobisher was considerably less impressed with Lopez's skill with the carbine. He came hurrying up.

'You boys surely know how to advertise!' he said. 'I'd be mighty obliged if we could just get the pair of you across the river. Somebody's sure to be here directly to look into that bang you caused.'

Since there was no longer anything to detain them in the United States Colonel Lopez readily agreed to this proposal. He allowed the young soldier to be ferried over the Rio Grande before climbing into the hoist himself and being pulled across the river by Jake Frobisher.

As he was slowly jerked and dragged along the rope Lopez reflected that he had done all that a man of honour could do. The Emperor had ordered him to discourage the smuggling of arms across the border and he had surely done that. If he wished, he could resign his commission now and become a private citizen within a matter of minutes. It was also a satisfaction to him that he had prevented at least a few of those devils of Confederates from entering his country and setting up their homes there.

As he neared the Mexican side of the river Lopez realied that he had given little thought to what might be done with the six men he had brought with him from the fort at Cueda. Would they wish to return to their duties with the Imperial army, or might they wish to desert and join the rebels? Whatever they wished, the colonel knew that he was responsible for them and could make no final decision about his own future until he had learned what their views were and had either seen them safe back to their garrison or otherwise settled. As he swung ashore Lopez thought that, for all concerned, the less delay in finding out what these young fellows wanted the better.

Jake Frobisher was in a great hurry to untie the rope from the tree to which it was attached. Like his brother, he was in terror of soldiers arriving on either bank of the river and blaming him and his brother for massacres, aiding rebels, murder, smuggling and the Lord knew what else. At the very least he needed to submerge the rope and cover up any evidence of the smuggling activities.

On the other bank Pete Frobisher was also frantically engaged in hiding evidence. As soon as Colonel Lopez had been safely landed Pete Frobisher signalled to his brother with the flags, sending a brief message to the effect that they should leave their homes at least temporarily, and ride to the ferry to see what they might do next.

It was indeed in the midst of these efforts by the Frobisher brothers to save their business interests – and perhaps even their very lives – that there came the thundering of hoofs and a party of heavily armed riders appeared on the ridge of high ground overlooking Jake Frobisher's home. There were perhaps twenty men in the party and they all, to Jake's eyes at least, looked as though they meant murder.

He knew two of them; they were men with whom he had in the past conducted a little business in the smuggling line. From this Frobisher took it that all the men were members of Juarez's rebel army. Although he was pretty sure that these fellows had not come here to do him any harm, it was still an alarming situation because he was now certain-sure that those he had lately brought over the river were actually soldiers of Maximilian. How if the two parties took to fighting, with him right slap-bang in the middle of their disputations?

Surreptitiously and doing his damnedest not to attract undue attention to himself, Jake Frobisher began to back slowly away from the scene, so that he would not be quite so apt to get caught in the cross-fire if things turned hot.

The colonel had not yet had the chance to canvass the men he had been travelling with upon their political views; therefore he did not know what would be their reaction to the rebels, for so he took them to be. The body of riders trotted down the slope towards them, their faces grim and unfriendly. They surrounded Lopez and his men. One whom he took to be their leader rode forward a little:

'Who are you men?' he asked, speaking in Spanish. 'Whom do you serve, the Austrian dog or the true leader of our people?'

This was setting the case out as plainly as anybody might wish. Despite the delicacy of his position Colonel Lopez almost smiled at such bluntness. Instead, however, he assumed a grave expression.

'I am Colonel Miguel Valentin de Lopez,' he replied, 'late of the Imperial Army. His Excellency the President invited me to take command of his army and I am now prepared to accept this most gracious invitation.'

By the look on the fellow's face it seemed that he had heard of Colonel Lopez, for his attitude became subtly altered. Nevertheless he was still not altogether satisfied.

'This is all well and good, Colonel Lopez,' he replied. 'But what of these others? Whom do they

157

serve? Are they enemies or friends?'

'That is yet to be made known to me. But these men, whatever they choose, are under my protection. I have led them here and am answerable for them. Whoever they follow, I shall allow nobody to molest them until I have returned them to safety. Two are, as you may see, grievously injured.'

'We shall see what we shall see,' said the leader of the rebels. 'Let them now speak for their own selves. Say, you six, are you soldiers of the Emperor, or will you have as your leader Juarez, who is a true Mexican, like you?'

Things could hardly have been more tense. For Colonel Lopez everything, even his very life, now hung in the balance, depending entirely upon the reply that these six men would make to Juarez's men.

If they declared for the Imperial government these rebels would most likely be in favour of gunning them down on the spot. Lopez could not and would not tolerate any such action. The six soldiers had volunteered in good faith to serve with him and he for his part had a duty to take care of them. If it came to fighting now his duty was clear: he would have to protect these young men from anybody who would harm them.

The soldiers themselves seemed to be taken aback at the turn of events; their mouths gaped open in astonishment on hearing that their colonel was now to become leader of the rebels against whom they were supposed to be fighting. Lopez turned to address them.

'Do not fear, my men,' he told them. 'The choice lies freely upon you. If you will, you may return to your garrison at Cueda and I, Colonel Lopez, will guarantee your safety until you get there. Anybody who attempts to harm you will only be able to achieve that end when I am dead.'

As he spoke Lopez cast his eye around the ring of grim-faced men who surrounded him and the men from Cueda.

'Or, if you will be guided by me,' he continued, 'you will take another course. Some of you are, like me, true Mexican. Would you not rather have a Mexican ruling in Mexico City?

'What say you? Will you join me as soldiers of his Excellency, President Benito Juarez? If so, then you are all welcome to come with me now to join forces with these men to drive the foreigners from our land.'

The six soldiers spoke amongst themselves in low tones for a minute and arrived swiftly at a decision. Whether it was that they had conceived a great loyalty and affection for the colonel in the short time during which they had served under him, or whether it was because they were genuinely sick of the French invaders lording it over them, they decided without much hesitation upon their course.

It is possible that choosing the contrary option would undeniably have resulted in a bloody gun battle weighed with them and affected their choice, but for whatever reason – or combination of reasons

– they said that they wished to join Juarez. Lopez turned to the leader of the riders.

'Well then,' he said, 'we have six more men. Are you content?'

'I am content, Colonel. I know that our leader is anxious for you to be brought straight to him. We must make arrangements for these, our wounded.' The man sketched a salute and then turned to speak to his companions.

It was a relief to the colonel that he would not, after all, be compelled to fight against his own side. There now remained the weightier matter of riding south and deposing Maximilian. If he was any judge of such things, Lopez thought, they faced a hard autumn of campaigning and at least another year after that before they would be likely to ride in triumph through the capital.